A Wife

for

Alastair

WENDY MAY ANDREWS

Sparrow Ink
www.sparrowink.com

Secrets divide them. Could love build a bridge to help them overcome their deceptions?

Jane was full of resentment and fear when the man she had married by proxy came to collect her. She resented the circumstances that required her to marry and was afraid of being tied to a stranger, especially a stranger she had to keep secrets from.

Alastair Fredericksburg, Fred to his friends, had arranged successful proxy marriages for a few of his friends but still had mixed feelings about marriage due to his sister's unhappy union. He was understandably hesitant when his friends Ella and Carter McLain contacted him requesting that he arrange a marriage for their friend, Jane.

When a sudden inheritance that would solve many of his sister's problems is dependent on his marriage, Fred can't decide if it's the Devil or Providence watching out for him. Since Carter had already sent Jane's proxy, Fred quickly signs and registers their marriage. After making sure his sister was secure, Fred boarded the westbound train to claim his wife.

Jane was certain it was only the sweet wine they had been drinking that had caused her to agree to Ella's rash suggestion. She had failed to tell Ella of the secrets that made her an ineligible match for Alastair Fredericksburg. Would she be able to keep her secrets from her new husband? And could they ever be happy while divided by deception?

Dedication

In this story, Jane has a huge secret that she's keeping from her new husband she's just met. I believe communication is the key to any successful relationship. But it's most definitely not always easy. This book is dedicated to everyone learning to share their thoughts and feelings. Hopefully witnessing Alastair and Jane's struggles will help you find your own path to success.

Acknowledgements

I need to thank my wonderful beta readers. Especially this time! The manuscript they had to start with was a hot mess. Thank you Marlene, Suzanne, Monique, Alfred, and Christina. You are the best. Without your help and suggestions, this book wouldn't have made it.

Thanks to my editor, Julie Sherwood, who is great at dealing with my mixed up Canadian spelling and lack of comma knowledge. Any mistakes left behind are completely my fault.

The lovely cover on this book is the results of a collaboration between *Envision Literary Photography* and Les at *GermanCreative*

Chapter One

"What do you mean she's not here?"

Fred stared at his good friend. They hadn't seen each other in person in several years, but Carter was one of his best friends. They had known each other as boys and gone to University together. At least until Carter had left school to strike out on his own and seek his own future away from the hierarchy of the East. He had done well for himself. But Fred couldn't allow himself to be distracted by such thoughts.

"I wrote, telling you, and her, that I was on my way. Why did she not wait? Did she not trust that our marriage would protect her from her sister?"

Fred noticed Ella, Carter's wife, biting her lip. "I rather think it was your imminent arrival that set her off."

"I beg your pardon?" Fred wanted to yell at her, but she was such a sweet, delicate woman, he didn't have it in him. But what she was saying led him to believe his brand new wife, whom he hadn't yet even met, had left at the thought of meeting him, not due to her fear of her sister's machinations.

"I'm sorry," Ella said in a low tone as tears trembled in her eyes. "I thought we were doing you a favor, not a disservice, when we asked you to find her a husband and you decided to marry her yourself. But I fear we've done you wrong even though we owe you so much."

Fred watched in frustration as Carter put his arm around his wife and said, "You couldn't have possibly known she would run off like that. I certainly didn't, and I've known her and her family far longer than you have."

"But I was the one spending so much time with her. I should have realized something wasn't right. And I did know she was disturbed by something, but I just thought it was how viciously angry her sister had become over the news that she could no longer force Jane into marriage with Avery Flynn. I thought Jane would feel safe now that Fred was on the way. I thought it was nerves. I'm so very sorry, Fred."

"Don't get yourself worked up, Ella, it can't possibly be good for you." Fred's gaze glanced briefly to the growing belly she couldn't hide and actually felt a smile tug at his lips when the woman touched it protectively. There was just something about a mother's love that Fred found so appealing. Maybe because he had lost his mother at a young age and had felt the need to take on that role with his sister. The thought of his sister hardened his resolve.

"When was the last time you saw her?"

"Yesterday. She said she wanted to be as fresh as possible for your arrival, so she retired very early. Her explanation seemed sensible, so I didn't even check on her before I retired for the night."

"And I, of course, didn't either," Carter interjected.

"So, you can have no way of knowing when exactly she left or where she might have been heading?"

"None whatsoever," Ella answered glumly while Carter nodded. "We checked with her sister this morning when we realized Jane was gone."

Fred raised his eyebrows. "That can't have been a pleasant experience."

Ella actually smiled. "I think the poor woman is seriously ill. She laughed when we told her we thought Jane was missing and were worried about her. I don't think she knows anything. At least nothing that could be in the least helpful."

"She might know where Jane would have gone, mightn't she? Or to whom she might go for help."

Ella didn't look convinced. "I don't think so. It doesn't seem as though Jane had anyone but us to turn to. Unless she was to go back to Boston. But I was always under the impression that she didn't consider that to be an option. That was why she was so very terrified by her sister's efforts to marry her off to Avery Flynn. She didn't feel she had anywhere to turn. Which is why she sent you her proxy."

"Which she no longer seems to be happy about."

"There has to be some sort of explanation."

"I'm sure there is," Fred replied, "but not an explanation we are about to get any time too soon, from the looks of things. I don't even know what she looks like, so I'm not completely certain how I shall even search for her."

Ella and Carter exchanged a glance. The type that made Fred feel isolated. The kind of glance that spoke of understanding, without the need for words. Fred was happy for them, but it made him all the more lonely. If only he had found a wife eagerly waiting for him. He would be on the way to being able to share glances like that himself rather than feeling isolated and rejected once more. Fred pulled his thoughts into order. It wouldn't do to fall into a melancholy now. He had a bride to find. Unfortunately, he was already married to the girl. What a complete mess.

~ ~ ~

Jane looked around the crowded train station. She had thought leaving in the night would have benefited her. She had hoped to be far from here long before now. She hadn't accounted for the fact that the schedule didn't run upon her insistence. She could hear the time ticking by both literally and figuratively. There was a large clock beside her. The tick-tick-tick was driving her mad, reminding her of the diminishing chances of her escape.

She had hidden in the cloakroom when the train arrived, even though she knew her groom had no idea what she looked like. It had been an instinctive reaction. One of self-preservation. And that right there was the saddest commentary on the farce that her life had become. She had hidden in the cloakroom to avoid her brand new husband. Jane heaved a heavy sigh.

She acknowledged the fact that her life had been spiraling out of control for the past several years. Ever since her mother had died, really. That was when she had been pulled out of school. Her father had never believed in educating his daughters. He had only agreed in order to pacify his wife. Once she was no longer around, he didn't see the need to continue.

Jane had pleaded with her father, begging him, based on his late wife's wishes, to leave her in school. She had only been two years away from completing the basic education. She had loved learning. If she could have had her wish, she would have continued school indefinitely. From what she had heard, there was a University in Boston that was welcoming female students. But one needed at minimum the most basic education before being able to continue on to higher education, she was sure.

Her lack of learning was just one of the things that made her feel inferior. She never felt comfortable with most other people. And now she was married to Alastair Fredericksburg. How was that to be born? He was the most attractive man she had ever laid eyes upon. Even better looking than Carter McLain, in her opinion. She would never tell Ella that, of course, but that was her view on the subject, and there wasn't anything that was likely to persuade her otherwise.

Jane allowed her mind to drift to the last time she had seen Mr. Fredericksburg. His brown hair had seemed to glow in the sunlight, flashing golden and auburn in the bright light of day. He was the picture of health. Tall, lean, and strong beneath his fashionable clothes. His erect carriage and strong hands had been such a stark contrast to her father's stooped, wasting posture.

She didn't like to think of her father. Not that he had been the worst she had ever heard of. He had never raised his fists against her or any of her siblings. But he had never had an encouraging word to offer, either. And despite his lack of violence, he had raised the family with a figurative iron fist, never willing to listen to reasoning of any sort.

He had refused to comfort any of them, as well. Their mother's death had been the first, but they had lost siblings as well. It seemed the man had shrunk with each one. Finally, he had sent Jane out to work. That was his final explanation as to why she couldn't continue in school. She needed to help support the family. Why she had to, and not her older brothers, was a mystery for Jane, but she had obeyed. And all her dreams had finally drifted away. Or so she had thought. They had rekindled momentarily when Ella had spoken of arranging a husband by proxy. Ella's belief that it would solve all Jane's problems had been momentarily contagious. But such miracles did not happen to her. Ella's success was surely a lucky happenstance.

Jane was, of course, happy for Ella and Carter. She didn't begrudge them their happiness for the briefest moment. Jane didn't think she would have been happy with Carter herself, despite Phoebe's conviction that she ought to have married him. She still shook her head with disbelief whenever she thought of her sister's plans. Phoebe had sent for her from Boston, it was well over a year ago, now.

Jane had been so excited when she had received her sister's message. She had been so sure that her luck was finally changing. Finally, one of her family cared for her and would rescue her from the drudgery that was her life. But when she had arrived, it had become obvious very quickly that her sister wasn't well. It was tragic, really, and Jane felt sorry for her sister most of the time.

Phoebe was her older sister, and Jane tried to respect her and care for her. But her crazy ideas were hard to cope with. Jane should have known. Phoebe had always had crazy ideas. They had just been a little better controlled when she was younger.

But how Phoebe had thought to force Carter to agree to marry Jane, she would never know. Perhaps Phoebe had just figured that he would be desperate for a wife being stuck out in the wilds of Missouri. But Carter was a resourceful man. He wouldn't have allowed such a consideration to force him into anything.

Phoebe hadn't wanted to accept that, though. She was determined to arrange an advantageous marriage for Jane. Jane still wasn't sure why her sister was so determined to get her married. There didn't seem to be anything much in it for her, but Phoebe was bound and determined. So much so that she had been making every effort to force Jane into marrying Avery Flynn. Which is why she had agreed to Ella's plan to send for a more appropriate groom from Boston.

But now that Jane was actually married, she had panicked. What would a well-to-do man from Boston want with her? She hadn't even finished her schooling. It would have been better for her to marry one of the townsfolk here in Missouri. Or even Avery Flynn. Maybe he wasn't so very bad. There must be some redeeming qualities to him, surely, or her sister wouldn't have been so insistent. But Jane couldn't agree to that arrangement. And she hadn't realized Ella would marry her off to Alastair Fredericksburg. Jane stifled a shudder. She should have known she was doomed.

So here she was, waiting for the train. She really ought to have gotten on the one Mr. Fredericksburg had gotten off. But it was heading further west. What she didn't want was somewhere even more primitive than where she already was. Jane had thought that one of the growing cities between here and Boston would be a good place for her to be able to hide and make a new life for herself.

As she sat there staring off into space, her mind drifted back toward her new husband. His handsome appearance was only one of the many things to recommend him. And only one of the many that made her desperate to get away from him. She didn't deserve such a catch; that was for certain. Jane shook her head. She really should have agreed to the marriage her sister wanted for her. She didn't deserve better.

Jane felt a catch in her throat and took herself to task. Now was not the time to give in to her emotions. She had clearly been spending far too much time with Ella St. Clair McLain. It had given her too many ideas. Ella was always going on about deserving the best in life. And connecting with your feelings.

Feelings had never gotten Jane very far, at least not since her mother's death. Feelings were a luxury she couldn't afford as she had worked, scrubbing floors and latrines, in the homes of her former friends after her circumstances had reversed so spectacularly. Her father's grief had made it impossible for him to continue his banking career. In the end, she had done whatever was necessary to keep food on the table. Well, she temporized, within reason.

She had managed to hold onto her moral compass despite the hardships she had faced. Sometimes she wondered why she had bothered, but it felt like she was holding onto the last vestige of her former self. It had been a comfort on the coldest, early morning as she had made her way to work. She had been confident she was doing the right thing. Jane believed her mother would have nodded in approval if she had been able to see her. Of course, her mother would have been devastated to know she had gone into service. Jane's mother had been from an old wealthy family. But they had turned their backs on Jane and the rest of her family after her mother died.

Sighing again, Jane gazed out the window, willing a train to appear in the station. She could have walked to the next station at this rate. She should have. She was like a sitting duck waiting here, as though she wanted to be caught. Jane wondered if her husband would even know her if he saw her. But if Ella or Carter were looking for her, surely this would be one of the first places they would ask about her.

She glanced around the waiting room once more. There weren't many people waiting for the train. It wasn't the time of year that people left. More often they were arriving in droves, now that the spring thaw had finally set in earnest.

Jane thought once more about her new husband. What would he be thinking? Would he be relieved that he wasn't actually saddled with her? Could he have their marriage cancelled somehow? He could claim she had abandoned him. Not that such a virile man would want to make such a claim, but it would be true, and surely there was a legal precedent for it.

She hadn't paid as close attention as she should have when Carter was explaining all the legalities of their situation, but she was fairly certain they had to take up communal residence at least for some time period. But they were well and truly married, she knew that. Carter had explained that there had been serious reasons for Mr. Fredericksburg to seek the marriage. Jane hoped her desertion didn't mess with his plans.

Jane bit her lip. What if it did? She would have done wrong to two members of that family, in that case. Would she be able to live with herself? She sighed again and once more felt tears trembling on her lashes. Her feelings were pressing against her breastbone. How she wished her mother were there to advise her. But that was an empty wish that she had been dreaming of for years. She had to figure this out for herself.

With a deep sigh, she got to her feet. She would return to the McLains'. Perhaps they could advise her. Or she could confess everything, and her husband could choose to reject her. She would be no further behind but would have a clearer conscience. She would be able to comfort herself that she had done the right thing. It was cold comfort, but she would take comfort wherever she could.

Stepping from the station, she felt her feet weighted down with her dread. But she determined to follow through. If she wasn't rejected by the handsome man, she would work her hardest to be the best wife she possibly could be. She knew how to work hard. She had an entire history of doing so. Surely, being a wife couldn't be much more difficult than what she had already faced. And she tried not to be too optimistic, but there was a possibility that it might even be easier than some situations she had faced. But it would be better not to have her expectations too high.

Her feet dragged. It had seemed long enough in the dead of night, but walking the distance between the station and the McLains' a second time was becoming excruciating. And the first time, she had felt as though she were escaping. Now, on the return trip, her heart filled with dread and it added weight to her feet and legs. She hoped she could make it before dark settled in once more. Jane castigated herself for not having the foresight to bring food along. What had she been thinking? She hadn't been; more's the pity.

Just when she thought she couldn't go on, a carriage came into view. Jane wondered if she had conjured the sight. Then she wished it would disappear, when she realized it was her husband. She probably looked a sight. Jane had very little confidence in her appearance at the best of times, but she was certain that now, worn out from two very long walks and a day without eating, she must look frightful. It was all a bit much. She felt the edges of her consciousness turning fuzzy, but she refused to give in to the weakness. Clenching her teeth, she stepped off the road to get out of his way as he pulled the carriage to a halt beside her.

Chapter Two

red gazed at the woman before him. She looked dainty and fragile and nothing like the woman he had spoken to earlier today, but from Ella's description, he was nearly certain this was his wife. She looked as though the next wind would carry her away. She was the most beautiful creature he had ever laid eyes on.

Part of him wanted to pull her into his arms and comfort her, as he could clearly see a war taking place on her face. But the other part of him wanted to yell at her for being so foolish as to run away in the middle of the night. And to walk so very far on her own. Had she no concern for her own safety? Or had she dreaded their marriage so much that she would rather risk life and limb?

That thought held him paralyzed. He had thought he was doing her a favor in marrying her. Or rather they were doing each other a service through their marriage by proxy. The fact that she had run away when she knew he would be arriving led him to believe she didn't view it in quite the same manner.

"Miss Cosburn?" he asked, even though he wanted to call her Mrs. Fredericksburg.

"Yes?"

"I'm Alastair Fredericksburg. My friends call me Fred. I believe I'm your husband."

If it were possible, her face turned a whiter shade of pale, and Fred was almost certain she was going to topple over, but she stiffened her spine and remained upright. He admired the steel that was clearly evident in her, despite her attack of nerves over their marriage.

"It's a pleasure to make your acquaintance," she answered him with a thin voice that barely breathed past her whitened lips.

"It doesn't seem to me that it is a pleasure for you, since you saw fit to run away rather than make my acquaintance."

He shouldn't have goaded her. She took a step back and leaned against the tree near the road. She was such a slip of a thing that she barely moved the scrawny tree.

"I needed a few minutes to think things over, sir. I apologize for my rudeness."

"No need to apologize to me, although Ella and Carter might have some words for you. It's not all that surprising that you had a few second thoughts about wedding a stranger."

He could see timidity shivering all around her, but she met his gaze and spoke despite it. "Did you have second thoughts?"

"I did all my second thinking before signing the paperwork," was all he bothered to answer. It was too complicated to explain it all right now when she was clearly at the end of her energy. "Never mind about that, though. It seems your energy is about to give out on you. Can I help you up into the wagon? I'm fairly certain the McLains will have some sort of food prepared for us. Ella seemed like she was going to fill the house with her cooking today. She said it gave her something to do while she worried about you."

He probably shouldn't have said that either. The girl's moan was low but clearly audible. "I shouldn't have run out like that. I should have realized she would worry. Do you think it has harmed the babe?"

Fred appreciated that she was expressing concern for others. He had wondered momentarily if she was dreadfully selfish when he turned up and she was nowhere to be found. While she might still be, at least she was showing more concern for someone other than herself.

"Carter has been keeping her calm throughout the day, as much as possible, but it will be good for her to know that you are well."

The girl nodded and climbed slowly into the carriage, being careful to stay well away from him.

"Might I ask where you have been?"

Her cheeks colored, but he couldn't tell if it was from anger or embarrassment.

"I was at the train station."

He stared at her blankly. "In Council Bluffs?"

Now she stared at him as though he were a simpleton. "Yes, I know of no other station close by."

"But that's just it — it isn't close by. How did you get there? And back here? Did someone give you a ride?"

"No, it was the middle of the night. There was no one about for me to ask."

"You walked all the way to the train station in the middle of the night?"

"Well it took all night, so I guess I wouldn't say the middle of the night."

Fred wasn't certain if she were trying to be funny or not and stared at her to ascertain her meaning. One corner of her mouth lifted in what appeared to be a self-deprecating smile.

"I guess it's not the time to make light of the situation, is it?"

She looked away as though she couldn't meet his gaze but then brought her face back toward his, took a deep breath, and brought her eyes to meet his. He appreciated that it appeared to be a brave act.

"I apologize, sir, I didn't mean to cause trouble or upset. I will apologize to Ella and Carter as soon as we arrive there. They have been nothing but kindness toward me, despite what my sister tried to do to them. I owe them better than I did."

Fred's heart went out to her. The beautiful, young woman clearly had a gentle soul. She had probably just become overwhelmed with nerves. It was perfectly understandable under the circumstances, he supposed. She might never have learned how to express her concerns, judging from the harpy who was her sister. He felt the urge to reach out and clasp the hands that were clenched tightly in her lap in an effort to offer comfort but was uncertain if it would be a welcomed gesture at this point in their acquaintance. He settled for patting her on the shoulder but could feel her slight flinch under his hand, so he didn't prolong the contact. He sighed. This was going to take more effort than he had thought it would.

Perhaps it had been arrogant or merely short sighted of him, but he had thought all he needed to do was show up and claim his bride, and she would fall in with his plans immediately. His history of arranging brides by proxy for his friends had lead him to believe it was as easy as riding a horse, but then he remembered the few times he had fallen off as a boy and realized that maybe his analogy was a good one. Eventually it would become second nature, but there might be a couple bumps in the road at the beginning. Fred resolved to ask Carter how he and Ella had adjusted to their marriage so easily. And while he was at it, perhaps he would wire Ransom and ask if he and Hannah could come for a visit. They were only a state away. Perhaps they could ride the train and meet up for a few days. He should probably check with Carter and Ella before making such plans.

Fred had been hoping to collect his bride and return to the city right away, but it might help them both transition if they could get to know one another in the company of friends. He suddenly remembered his wife had said she was on her way to the train station.

"Had you a particular destination in mind when you reached the station? Or you just thought to get on the first one that arrived?"

He heard her sigh and almost smiled.

"I had a destination. Perhaps it would have been wise to catch the first one. It was the one you arrived on. I hid in the luggage room while you got off. Not that you would have known me, but fear does strange things to otherwise sensible people."

"That it does," he agreed in a cheerful tone. "Were you hoping to visit friends? I could accompany you if you wish to go somewhere particularly. Or I could take you to visit my friends. Has Carter ever mentioned Ransom Delaney to you? We all went to school together. I haven't seen him in years. He and his wife and family live just a state away."

Once again that brought her gaze sharply to his face. He could feel her searching his gaze as though trying to ascertain his meaning. Fred tried to keep his face as relaxed as possible, unsure what she might be reading there or what she was even looking for. It wasn't a complicated sentence, he hadn't thought.

"You're being terrible kind to me," she stated. "Aren't you angry that I ran away?"

"Angry? No. You had an attack of nerves, didn't you?"

She nodded but didn't say anything.

"It would have been better if you had chosen to discuss your feelings with someone. Me preferably, of course," he said with a smile but hurried on at the stricken expression upon her face. "Or Ella. I believe you two are friends. I don't know her really well, but she's best friends with my sister. I know she can keep a confidence."

Fred couldn't interpret the brief expression that flitted across Jane's face when he mentioned his sister and her friendship with Ella but he plowed on.

"But, no, I'm not angry with you at all."

She offered him a half smile and nodded, looking away from him once more.

"You said you hid while I disembarked. So, you actually managed to walk all the way to the station? You must be exhausted! And you had made it almost all the way back! Did you have help returning?"

Jane sighed again. "No, I walked the entire way. I'm a good walker. Fast. It isn't that difficult. And you can think all sorts of things while you walk, especially if you're by yourself, so it isn't such a terrible thing. But, yes, I am rather tired. I, of course, didn't sleep last night. And, stupidly, I didn't think to take any food with me, not that I would want to take Ella's provisions, but I'm sure she wouldn't have begrudged me an apple or two. But in my haste, I didn't even take that. So, I'm even more hungry than I am tired."

"Why didn't you buy something to eat while you were in Council Bluffs or when you passed through Trader's Point?" He hadn't paid much attention when he was there, but the town with the train station should have had several places she could have purchased food, and even the smaller town would have one or two.

Her delicate features colored once more, and her shoulder lifted in a half shrug. "I spent all my money on my ticket."

"Which you haven't even used." Fred didn't mean to sound censorious, but he was now concerned that the girl truly might faint on him before he got her back to Carter's property. Being a city man, he wasn't so familiar with the wagon he was driving, and he didn't know the animals at all. He wasn't certain he would be able to catch a fainting woman and control a moving wagon at the same time.

Jane would no longer meet his gaze, and her voice was barely audible as she said, "The station master assured me that I could use my ticket another day, but he would subtract a bit for a fee for the trouble. But I won't lose the entirety of the cost of the ticket. I'm sorry."

"No need to apologize," Fred said once more, wishing they were starting on a different foot. "I shouldn't have been short with you. I'm more concerned for you than I expected to be, and that led me to snap. Are you going to be able to manage until we get there? I don't have anything with me."

"I'll be fine. Hunger isn't deadly."

"It can be," he argued.

"One or two days without food doesn't do much harm."

Fred blinked. She sounded as though she were speaking from experience. He was just about to question her further when she surprised him with her question.

"Where were you going when you came across me?"

"I was looking for you."

Her eyebrows rose, and a smile touched her pale lips. "You were?"

"Of course, I was! We were worried about you."

She hung her head, and her smile died. "I know. I'm sorry."

"Never mind with the apologies. At least you were coming back. What made you change your mind?"

What appeared to be dozens of conflicting emotions crossed her face one after the other. Fred couldn't catch them, but he was left with the impression that she was still torn on the subject. He waited to hear what she would give as way of explanation.

She gave him that cute, one shouldered shrug once more. "I didn't want to inconvenience you."

Fred threw back his head and laughed. He couldn't help himself, even though she didn't look most pleased at his amusement.

"I'm sorry, my dear, I promise I'm not laughing at you. But from my perspective, marriage isn't all that convenient. So, it just sounded funny when you said it like that."

She shrugged again. "I guess I should have said I didn't want to inconvenience you further. Saving me by marrying me, already was an inconvenience, I'm sure. And then to come all this way, which you needn't have done. I could have come to you."

Fred raised his eyebrows at her. "Really? You would have come to me? You ran away when you found out I was coming to you."

Jane smiled. "True. But perhaps action would have helped me feel like I had control over my life. That's actually why I came back. Leaving and buying the train ticket with my last few coins made me feel less at the mercy of fate and others. So, coming to you might have done the same."

"Well, I wasn't to know that," Fred excused.

His wife smiled. "Of course, you weren't. I didn't know it either until just now."

Fred continued. "And actually, I should explain to you that while marriage might not be so convenient, our marriage wasn't merely to save you. It was a mutually beneficial arrangement, I can assure you."

Now her eyes were wide, reminding him of a baby owl. "How could I benefit you?"

Wishing he hadn't brought up the subject, wanting to wait until they knew each other better, Fred tentatively patted her on the shoulder once more. "I'll explain it to you later," he assured her. He was filled with gratitude that the McLains' house had come into view, saving him from the awkward conversation. "We've arrived, and we need to get you fed before you fall over from your hunger."

She scoffed. "I'm not such a weakling." But then followed up on her words by needing to cling to the wagon as she climbed down.

Ella hurried from the house and gathered Jane into her outstretched arms. "You poor girl, you must be exhausted. We've been worried sick about you, you silly thing. Come inside, and I'll feed you up properly."

Fred watched with fascination. The Ella St. Clair he had known in Boston had been a city girl from the crown of her head down to the tips of her toes. And he hadn't thought she had a motherly bone in her body. But now, watching her cluck over the "girl" who couldn't be any younger than she was, he could see that she was going to be an excellent mother to the baby she was going to have.

Fred felt his chest clench with what was most likely envy as he watched his old friend Carter follow after his wife and her charge. Fred felt excluded from the familial scene, even though it was actually his wife being borne along by the pair. At least she was his wife on paper. She was clearly reluctant to take on the role in actuality. At least she came back. He would have to be satisfied with that.

I didn't want to inconvenience you. What did that say about the young woman who was his wife? Her only concern was to not be an inconvenience. Clearly, she wasn't from a loving household, judging from what he had seen of her sister. He wondered if mental illness ran in the family. It was a little late to worry about that now that they were legally committed to one another. Of course, he could always get that reversed, but that seemed churlish at this point. They had committed to one another in good faith. They would have to try to make the most of it.

At least she had come back. He would have to focus on that one bright thought. She hadn't abandoned her commitments, even if she had succumbed to a moment of nerves. And she had clearly been concerned for Ella and her baby. And the McLains spoke highly of her. And he had given his word.

This last thought was the most important. He prided himself deeply on being a man of his word. And the financial windfall that had accompanied his marriage made it possible for him to provide for his sister. For that alone he owed his loyalty to the young woman who was his wife. She may never fully comprehend the debt he owed her. He needed to set himself to the task of making sure she had a good life. Starting with making sure she was fed.

This prompted his feet to finally set themselves in motion, and he hurried after the trio who had gone ahead of him.

Chapter Three

Jane felt tears prickling at the backs of her eyes. She didn't want to give in to the weakness, but her tired and hungry state was making it more difficult than usual. Everyone was being extraordinarily kind to her, considering how much trouble she was being. It made her decidedly uncomfortable. She never should have walked away in the first place. Then she wouldn't be in this predicament.

Looking around at the three faces watching her expectantly, Jane couldn't help the trembling smile that stretched her lips.

"You three are making me feel like an exhibition. Why don't you eat, too, and then it won't feel so very awkward for me?"

"Of course, how silly of me," Ella responded immediately. "I am just so relieved to have you back." The other woman giggled. "Which is ridiculous when you think about the fact that you'll be leaving again soon, with Fred, back to Boston. But at least then I'll know for sure you're safe and sound. And I'll be able to anticipate letters from you. You *will* write, won't you?"

Jane knew her friend had no intention of making her uncomfortable with her words. There was no way for the gracious and graceful Mrs. Ella McLain to know that her guest hadn't finished her schooling, since Jane had kept that a tightly guarded secret. Oh, she knew how to write, of course, but she never felt as though her words were good enough. What could she possibly write about to her friend? If Jane were returning to the city, her life and that of her friend would be worlds apart.

But the only appropriate answer was, "Of course, I will." She only hoped it wasn't a lie as she swallowed it down with the delicious biscuit her friend had baked.

"Ella, these biscuits are just like Sybil's cook bakes, which are the best biscuits I've ever tasted. I had no idea you were such a great cook."

Ella's smile was wide as she accepted his compliment. "They should taste like Cook's biscuits. That's who I learned from."

"Really? I haven't heard this story."

"When you arranged for me to come out here to be Carter's wife, I needed a crash course in the kitchen. Your sister's cook was kind enough to agree to help me. And she gave me all her simplest recipes. Sybil has been sending me recipes and instructions from the cook in almost every letter she sends. And then she reads my tales of success and failure to the kitchen staff. It amuses them."

All four at the table laughed, although Jane had to clear her throat to get it out. She had been cooking since she was a youngster. It wasn't an accomplishment. But Ella's cooking was delicious. And she had only learned how less than two years ago, so

Jane supposed it was an accomplishment for Ella, since she had always had servants in the past.

Suddenly, Jane had a stunning thought. If her husband's sister had servants, did he as well? Would they? Her breath caught in her throat, and she was once again feeling slightly faint. Servants! Just the thought of not having to slave for others in order to keep food on the table made her light in the head. Of course, while she had been living with her sister, she hadn't actually been earning an income, although her sister had expected her to work as hard as she ever had back in the city.

And while she had been staying with the McLains ever since Phoebe had found out she was a married woman and had thus kicked her out of her house in a furious rage, Jane had felt obligated to work as hard as possible to earn her keep. Jane had been able to ignore Ella's constant insistence that she needn't do so much, since the other woman had often grown tired and napped midafternoon. Of course, her stay with the McLains had been the most idyllic time of her life since her mother's death. The thought that she could actually live like that with her new husband was more than she had even considered when she had imagined remaining married to the handsome Alastair Fredericksburg.

If she could keep him from finding out about her connection to his sister's problems. It was likely best if most of her own background were kept to herself. She knew Fred was a well-educated man; she would hate for him to find out she hadn't even finished the basic education. And that she had been a servant. She had thought she had caught him looking at her with admiration a time or two but had discounted the idea as preposterous. Though she had enjoyed the possibility. She could be certain he would never look at her that way again if he knew her full history.

Could she live a lie? Was it even a lie if it were just a matter of not sharing all the information? Not really, right? If he didn't ask directly, she wasn't obliged to tell him everything, was she? Jane chewed her lip. She had prided herself on maintaining moral fortitude when she had lost everything else. She had never lied before and would hate to start now. But the thought of a comfortable future was so enticing. If he never asked, she wouldn't go into any unnecessary details about her life.

Thus decided, she braced herself for whatever was to come. Her stomach churned at the thought of deceiving her husband, but she ignored it. Besides, she hadn't told Ella and Carter everything, and it had never crossed her mind to imagine that she was being untruthful. *But they didn't marry you*, her conscience whispered. Jane ignored the silent voice and turned her attention back to the conversation that had been swirling around her while her thoughts were elsewhere.

"Sybil was furious with me for not bringing her with me," Fred was saying.

"Oh, that would have been lovely," Ella promptly replied. "I haven't seen her since I left Boston. How is she? Her most recent letter seemed mysterious. You have set up some sort of trust for her? It sounded as though she was beside herself with happiness. Is she increasing? I couldn't understand why her tone was so different."

"I'm not certain if she is with child or not, and to be honest, it isn't a thought I want to entertain about my sister. I know she would love to have children, but her husband has been less than genial at times, so I've been happy they hadn't brought youngsters into the world. I have managed to gain leverage over the man, and it has wrought remarkable changes in his behavior."

"That's wonderful. I felt terrible about leaving her behind with Horace when I left Boston, but I was no longer welcome in his home, despite Sybil's loyal friendship. I know he's her husband. And I know she even loves him. But to me he was rather vile and I hated to leave her behind. I'm surprised you were able to gain control of him, though. He didn't strike me as one who would allow anyone to have anything over him."

"If you find the right thing, anything is possible."

Fred's answer felt mysterious and intriguing. Jane wanted to ask questions but didn't feel equipped for the conversation.

"Tell me what is new with the two of you." Fred didn't seem any further inclined to discuss his sister or her husband, easily changing the subject.

Ella blushed. Jane sighed. Her hostess was such a pretty woman, fairly glowing with her pregnancy and joy. She gestured to her belly.

"Well, as you probably couldn't help but notice, we are going to be adding to the family shortly."

"That's wonderful. When is the happy occasion?"

"In about two months' time."

"Are there sufficient medical practitioners in these parts?" Fred's solicitous concern warmed Jane's heart even if it wasn't directed toward her. He was a caring man, an attractive quality to be certain. Not that she should be thinking that way, since she was keeping such a large secret from him. She needed to guard her heart.

Ella and Carter laughed. "Yes, Fred, I've seen a doctor. And there is a midwife in these parts who has a wonderful reputation. They say she hasn't lost a baby or mother in her entire career. I suspect that might be exaggerated, but I feel confident in her hands."

Jane was watching Fred closely and was surprised to see a wistful expression cross his face. Did the man want children of his own? Or did he want to live in the wilds of Missouri?

Chapter Four

Fred felt Jane's gaze as if it were a physical touch. It was disconcerting. How could he be so aware of the woman when they'd only just met? Was it because she was officially his and he felt a responsibility toward her as such? But no, he had never felt this aware of his sister, Sybil, and he had felt responsible for her since she was born. He doubted it was even her beauty, as he had met beautiful women before. One of whom was also sitting at the table. When he had first met Ella St. Clair, he had thought her one of the most beautiful women he had ever met, but he wasn't so very aware of her as he was of this Jane Cosburn. Jane Fredericksburg, now, he reminded himself.

A part of him wanted to meet her gaze, to let her know he knew she was watching him. But the poor girl was already such a mess of nerves he didn't want to add to her discomfort. He doubted her fears had righted themselves with her long walks; she had only gained control over them. Or at least felt her responsibility to live up to her word was greater than her fear.

Fred appreciated that sentiment. His word was of the utmost importance to him. He liked that she seemed to consider it important, too. And she had felt an obligation toward Ella and Carter. Hopefully, she would be able to develop warmer feelings toward him with time, but if they could start with feelings of commitment, they could work toward everything else.

But the young woman was clearly at the end of her abilities at the moment. From the corner of his eye, he could see she was barely able to keep her eyes open. The dark smudges below the bright blue gaze didn't detract from her beauty but definitely leant her an enhanced air of fragility. Fred didn't believe for a second that she was actually fragile; she merely looked it due to her fatigue. If she could walk the miles and miles to Council Bluffs, not once, but twice in the space of twenty-four hours, she was far stronger than she appeared. But now she needed some rest.

"I think it's time that we all retire," Fred said by way of interrupting the conversation Ella and Carter were trying to keep afloat. Neither of their guests were participating at this point, so he wasn't sure why they were making such an effort. Probably, Ella's ideas of societal expectation from her days in Boston, he thought with a small smile. She was such a city girl in her soul, despite her apparent adjustment to life on Carter's spread.

His words may not have been well thought out. If it were possible, his wife had paled further. Fred had meant to make it evident that he didn't expect her to fulfill certain marital obligations until they were better acquainted, but he hadn't found a way to bring that up yet.

"Is there somewhere I could sleep? I could even bunk down in your hayloft if there's nowhere free in here or with your men." He paused for a second and smiled as he saw, again from the corner of his eye, his wife almost wilt with relief. "I know we didn't discuss an extended stay, but I don't think we're going to be ready to head back to Boston for a few days yet."

Ella promptly spoke up. "You're always welcome in our home, Fred, and you can stay as long as you'd like." She exchanged a glance with her husband, and then her attention drifted to Jane. Fred wasn't sure what she was looking for in his wife or if she found it, but she turned back to him with what appeared to be forced cheerfulness. "You can have your choice of sleeping arrangements. There is room in the bunkhouse, as we haven't yet hired all the hands we'll need this spring, but I've heard the men saying that Bob is a noisy sleeper, so you're welcome to the hayloft if you think that might be more comfortable."

"Oh no, Ella, you mustn't send him to the barn. I could sleep in the barn, and he can take my room. I won't mind at all. It's nice and warm in there, and the animals are a comfort."

Fred couldn't believe his ears. His delicate little wife was offering her own bed for him. Not with her in it, of course, but she would rather put herself out than for him to do so. He appreciated her inclination, but there was no way he would allow her to make such a sacrifice.

"I sleep like a log, so I don't think Bob will disturb me in the least, thank you." He wasn't sure if that were completely true, but he didn't actually want either he or his wife to experience the hayloft. From the sounds of it, though, his wife had already experienced it and was willing to repeat the experience. He wouldn't stand for it though.

The expression on her face indicated she wanted to protest, and he was curious to hear what she might say, but then she met his gaze and snapped her lips shut before glancing away in obvious discomfort. He reached toward her and patted her shoulder.

This, too, was a new development for him. Along with his awareness of her, he felt the compulsion to touch her. It wasn't something he had ever been urged to do before. Not even with his sister, whom he loved dearly and would exchange hugs with or they would hold each other's arm as they walked. But this was different. From the moment he first clapped eyes on her, he had to fight the urge to pull Jane into his arms. It was disconcerting. He offered her a smile and was relieved to see her return it.

But then she seemed startled by their interaction and quickly got up from the table and excused herself, hurrying up the stairs. A moment later, there came the soft click as she shut her door. Fred wondered if her door had a lock on it. Not that he would ever consider forcing his presence upon her, but was that the sound he had heard? He turned his troubled gaze to his hosts, who were gazing at him expectantly.

Fred offered them what he hoped was a confident looking smile. "She's lovely."

Ella giggled. "She is, actually, but I'm afraid you haven't yet seen her good points. I truly am sorry, Fred. We should have realized there was more going on with her and prevented her from panicking."

"I don't know how you could have done that if she didn't want to confide in anyone," Fred answered reasonably. "Don't let it trouble you, Ella, I promise, I'm not going to hold a grudge against you or her. It all ended well, at least for now. But perhaps you could lock her in tonight somehow, in case she changes her mind."

The three shared a chuckle. Fred figured they didn't take him seriously. He was undecided if he had meant his words or not. He didn't know the woman and didn't know if she could be relied on. She hadn't actually expressly given her word that she wouldn't run again. Fred had the impression that she was usually the reliable sort despite her recent behavior. He was fairly certain Ella and Carter's experiences in life had made them pretty good judges of character, and they vouched for her. Regardless, there was nothing that could be done now. Hopefully the girl would be able to get a good, long sleep and they could deal with the issues in the morning. He, too, could use some rest. It had been a more stressful day than he had realized.

Fred needed to hold onto his wife for at least a while. He didn't savor the thought of divorce, but it wasn't impossible to obtain with the right lawyer. If his wife truly couldn't bear the thought of being married to him, he would try to set her free. But he needed to keep her at least until his own affairs were settled. And he couldn't allow anything to disturb the peace he had finally been able to restore for Sybil. He wouldn't force his wife to return to Boston if she truly didn't want to, but she would have to remain legally his for at least a while longer. She had given her word when she sent him her proxy, and he had every intention of making sure she kept it.

It would be something to confront tomorrow. Fred tried to clear it from his mind for the time being. There was no need to worry he would forget. It was his life now. And he would need all his wits about him in the morning. That is to say, as long as his wife didn't walk away in the middle of the night again.

Chapter Five

It had been his grumbling stomach that had awoken him. Fred had slept far later than was his wont. He supposed it made sense. He hadn't slept perfectly soundly on the train. The constant motion, while hypnotic, hadn't been as restful as he had expected. Fred was relieved that he hadn't noticed any noises coming from Bob or any of the men in the bunkhouse that night. And he had actually slept through any of their morning activity. Chasing after his wife yesterday must have exhausted him more than he realized.

The day had dawned bright and beautiful. Fred had never been this far west before and hadn't expected the scenery to be so very different than what he was used to. He had kept his head buried in books on the train ride, hoping to have most of his business finished up so he could concentrate on his wife during the ride back to Boston. Now, of course, he wasn't certain if he would be travelling back any time soon and if he would be doing so with a wife in tow or not. Either way, he would have to go to the telegraph office in Trader's Point and send some messages back to the city within the next day or two, whether they were heading east or not.

But now he needed to eat. Soon. Or he would be growly as a bear before long. Fred quickly made his way to the bucket of water sitting at the side of the room and cleaned himself up as best as he could. It wasn't the type of conditions he was used to, but he would like to think he wasn't such a stickler that he couldn't make do for at least a few days.

Before long, he was striding toward the house, as freshened as he could manage, ready to fill his stomach and face the day.

"You've been a slugabed, it would seem, Fred. Are you feeling all right? It's unusual for you to sleep so late. We didn't even have any spirits last night."

Fred laughed over Carter's comment. "I was more tired than I had realized. And I think the air out here might be thinner or something. I haven't slept that soundly in ages."

"I'm glad to hear Bob didn't disturb you. The man can be loud."

Fred laughed again. "What are you doing hovering about out here? Were you coming to fetch me?"

"No, just leaving space for the womenfolk to get their talking over with," Carter replied. "Ella's gotten me more aware of feelings than I ever thought I'd want to be, but I don't want to take on Jane's as well. I'm sorry if that makes me a terrible friend, Fred, but I think I'll draw the line there. That's your responsibility now, my friend."

Fred quirked his eyebrows and eyed the front door of the house. He needed to get in there to address his hunger, but he was no more eager to confront the women's feelings than Carter was. Then he remembered Jane's words the day before.

"Are there apples?"

Carter grinned. "You haven't eaten, yet, have you? Yes, there are apples in a bin in the shed. Let's go."

A few minutes later, Fred was happily munching on an apple as his friend and host fussed with some bridles.

"You seem remarkably happy here in the wilds."

"It suits me," Carter commented before looking at his guest quizzically. "Have you suspected I've been miserable all these years since I left the University to try my luck out here?"

"Not miserable, no, but I thought perhaps you were writing overly optimistic messages in an attempt to avoid admitting you had made a mistake in moving away and leaving me behind."

Carter laughed and Fred joined him. "Did you feel abandoned? You've always been welcome to join me, or start a spread of your own. Although, with the train being so regular now, it might be harder to set yourself up in as affordable a way as I did over the years."

Fred suppressed a shudder. "No, I am well and truly ensconced in the city. And now that I've gained my windfall, I'm even less inclined to leave than I ever was. Although buying a spread wouldn't be a difficult proposition, even though the fresh air smells lovely, I'll take the salty air of Boston, thank you. But I did miss you when you left school."

The two friends shared a glance of understanding.

"I've enjoyed receiving your letters. Thank you for being such an excellent correspondent. I hadn't expected it, I'll admit."

"What do you mean? Did you question my literacy?"

Carter guffawed. "Hardly. I went to school with you for years, remember? No, I just figured you would forget about your crazy friend who had gone west."

Fred shrugged. "I didn't have so very many friends. I couldn't afford to lose you, even if you left me. And I enjoyed your tales whenever you managed to actually write."

"In the early years, I was bone tired every night and up again a few hours later."

"You've done really well for yourself, though, so it seems it was worth it."

Carter nodded. "Especially now with the baby on the way." He paused for a moment, glancing out into the distance before fixing his friend with his serious gaze. "I know I've written my thanks for sending me Ella, but I want to thank you again. She is the brightest aspect of my life. I cannot thank you enough."

Fred felt uncomfortable under the weight of his friend's gratitude. "Well, since you know her story, you know you were doing her a favor as much as yourself, but I'm glad it turned out so well for both of you." He paused, cleared his throat and continued. "Speaking of that, might I ask how long it took for you to feel that it *had* turned out?"

Carter chuckled. "Are you trying to see the light at the end of this darkness?"

"Something like that. I don't regret marrying the girl. She seems to be a sensible chit, if you can look past the crazy choice of walking through the night to escape meeting me." Fred smiled slightly, looking out the open barn door. "But all the times I arranged proxy marriages for different friends or acquaintances, I didn't look past the immediate reasons the couple was marrying. It was terribly short sighted of me. Now, I've already reaped the reward of entering the marriage, but I'm left with the reality of life with a stranger. A very permanent and present stranger."

"Well, the good news is, she won't be a stranger for long," Carter began. "And from what I've heard, you have a track record of successful unions, so you're likely to be successful in your own."

"I doubt your reasoning. In all the previous cases, I knew something of both parties and fully trusted at least one of them."

Carter's brows rose. "Do you not trust yourself?"

"Well, of course I do, but I know nothing of Miss Cosburn."

Carter laughed once more. "Well, for starters, she's Mrs. Fredericksburg now, but since she's your wife, I dare say you have leave to use her first name."

Fred could feel heat in his face and knew he was blushing like a girl. "Of course. But you see, I know so little about her that I'm not even comfortable being on a first name basis with her."

Carter nodded. "I can tell you, when I picked up Ella at the train station, I questioned your judgment. She was just too pretty. I wondered how I could possibly keep her happy here on my spread. And I had less than no desire to return to Boston. But very quickly she set about making herself at home here, and I just fell for her."

"Well, I have every intention of returning to Boston. I won't have the luxury of wilderness to confine my wife to my sphere."

"You will have a week-long train ride in which to become better acquainted, for one thing, and you're welcome to stay here as long as you'd like, if you think it might help."

Fred nodded, but Carter continued. "As well, you mentioned you knew something of both parties when you've arranged marriages in the past and felt confident in their success because of that." Fred nodded again. "Do you trust my judgment? I know we haven't spent any time together in person in years, but we've remained friends. And despite her dreadful sister, I think Jane is a good girl that will make you an excellent wife. She has a few odd ideas and doesn't seem capable of sitting still, but Ella really enjoys her company."

"Thank you, McLain, that does give me some comfort. Do you know anything about her background?"

"Not really. Her brother-in-law, Jacob, had been a hand on my spread before he bought his own property and then went back east for a wife. As you know, we haven't had the best of times with Phoebe, but Jane seems to be cut from a different cloth than her sister. I think there has been tragedy in her past. I don't think she has parents, nor many siblings. From what I can tell, she's been responsible for herself for far longer than she should have. But it doesn't seem to have altered her brain like it has her sister. Now Phoebe is a case, and you'd be best keeping the two sisters far apart. Not that I think Jane would wish to spend prolonged time with her sister, but there might be a familial sense of obligation."

Fred nodded, a little frustrated that while this was useful information, it didn't actually tell him much about his wife's character. He did trust Carter McLain, though, and if he thought she was a good, reliable woman, Fred would take it on faith and do his best to treat his wife well. But he might wait a while before he trusted her with all the facts about his situation.

"As fascinating as it is watching you fidget with your leathers, I suppose I ought to gird myself and go in search of my wife. She wasn't in much shape to discuss our future yesterday. Hopefully she has rested and is willing to talk today. At least she didn't run off again in the night, which was something I feared as I was retiring last night."

Carter didn't bother answering, just grinned and waved his friend away.

Fred's feet were heavy as he headed toward the main house. Hopefully the women had talked themselves out by now and were in a frame of mind to accept his presence. Staring at the front door, he wondered if he should knock or walk in. He chose to knock.

Ella's face was wary as she opened the door but then broke into a grin when she saw him. "Come in, come in. No one ever knocks, so I was nervous to open the door," she explained with a chuckle. "Have you had anything to eat? You must be starving. It's nearly noon. Can you wait until the midday meal or would you like us to fry you an egg in the meantime? Or there's some bread you could have as well."

"I wouldn't want to put you to any trouble," Fred began but then his stomach grumbled, and he laughed as he felt heat splash his cheeks. "I had a couple apples, but apparently, that was insufficient."

"Not to worry. How about I fry you an egg? You can have it on a slice of bread. That will tie you over until we all eat but won't take more than two or three minutes, so it's no trouble at all."

"Thank you, Ella."

"It's the least I can do for you, truly. I owe you much." Her simple answer humbled him, and he couldn't form a reply.

Clearing his throat, Fred asked, "Has Miss Cosburn recovered from her exertions?"

Ella laughed. "Your wife, you mean? Yes, she too slept later than usual, but she has been working like a slave for a couple hours." At Fred's raised eyebrows Ella leaned closer and whispered, "I think it's nervous energy that makes her unable to sit still. She's lovely, but I wonder how she'll manage on the train."

The words were not reassuring to Fred. He appreciated a hard-working person but didn't expect his wife to make herself a slave. And if she couldn't sit still, the long ride back to Boston was likely to be torture for them both.

Ella must have realized somewhat the direction of his thoughts as she continued, "The good news is, she seems much more settled in her mind about being married to you. She feels that she put us all in an awkward position yesterday and feels dreadful about that, which is why she feels the need to scrub my floors. But she'll probably be open to talking with you, if you can catch her between chores. I might add, do not feel you are taking her away from necessary tasks, she did most of them the day before yesterday."

Fred smiled at his hostess as she placed a plate before him. While she had chattered, she had fried him the perfect egg. Fred couldn't imagine his sister ever doing such a thing and wondered what she would think if she saw her best friend doing it. This brought a grin to his face.

"I do believe Sybil needs to come for a visit. Now that train travel seems to be dependable, she just might be able to convince Horace to bring her."

Ella's face clouded. "That might make the visit a little less enjoyable," she commented.

Fred smiled and nodded. "Maybe he would allow her to come alone, but she might be nervous coming all this way by herself."

Ella laughed. "I did it, and it wasn't so dreadful. But I'll see if I can convince her."

As she was speaking, Fred's attention was caught toward the stairs, and he didn't hear if she said anything else. His wife was the prettiest woman he had ever seen. She wasn't dressed fashionably, and it didn't look like she was even trying to be attractive. She had herself covered nearly from head to toe in an ugly fabric that he hoped was to protect her clothing and hair underneath. Her cheeks were flushed, probably from the work she had been doing. Or maybe she was too hot under all that cloth. Whichever the case might be, she was stunning. A few tendrils were escaping the cover she had placed over her hair and they were curling in the heat of her exertion. Her eyes glowed bright blue against the color of her flushed cheeks.

It took every ounce of Fred's will power to keep him in his seat. He wanted to go to her. Part of him even wanted to pull her into his arms and comfort her for the anxiety he knew she still felt. But he feared even approaching her would cause her to withdraw into her nervous shell. He waited with bated breath, hoping she would come to him.

His patience was soon rewarded. He watched her gaze bouncing around the room as though she were trying to decide what to do with herself. Finally, she started unwinding herself from the fabric covering and walked toward where he was seated at the table.

"Good morning," she said with a shy smile and a low voice. "Did you sleep well?"

"I slept remarkably well. Much later than usual."

She smiled. "The air is different here, isn't it? I found I slept deeper when I first arrived. Then, too, is the fact that it's not comfortable to sleep on the train."

"True. I had thought to return right away, but I'm not looking forward to the return trip. Staying here for a few days certainly holds appeal."

Fred said this last bit, hoping for a reaction from her, hoping she would let him in on her thoughts on the matter.

After she glanced toward the kitchen, she seemed to realize that Ella had everything under control. She pulled a chair out from the table and gingerly sat on the edge of it.

"Did you have a room or just a seat on the train?"

Fred was disappointed that she wasn't responding to his statement, but was relieved that she seemed open to a discussion.

"I had a bunk, but didn't have a room to myself. Thankfully, the other gentleman in the room kept to himself and was quiet. We shared a room the entire way. He is going to try his luck on the coast."

"It's hard to believe you can travel all the way across the country now without taking a wagon and oxen."

Fred stifled a shudder. "I can't even imagine the challenges that would have entailed. My friend from the train said he would actually have to ride horseback some distance because there are no connecting train lines getting to his intended destination."

"He sounds the adventurous sort. I believe Carter travelled here before the trains came through, didn't he?"

"That's true. But he was a foolish teenager at the time."

The tinkle of laughter that came from her quickened his pulse and warmed his heart. He was delighted to know she had a sense of humor. And seemed to appreciate his.

"So, I take it you don't intend to pursue your new friend west?"

"Not unless I was forced to do so."

"Such as by chasing after a recalcitrant wife?" Her question was accompanied by a dimpling grin, so Fred didn't think she was threatening him with further desertion.

"I hope that is never put to the test," he answered in a prim tone, which brought another peel of laughter from the young woman. He turned the subject. "You were from Boston before moving to Trader's Point to be with your sister, weren't you?"

He hadn't expected that question to cause her discomfort, so he was surprised when she appeared to brace herself before answering with a soft, "Yes."

"Are you reluctant to return to the city?" he probed.

She shook her head. "Not particularly. There are some lovely things about living in the city."

"What do you miss most?" Fred was hoping she would look forward to accompanying him.

"The salty air, I think."

Fred laughed. "I was just talking about that with Carter this morning. The air here smells sweet, which is nice, but I miss the salt already."

Jane nodded. "And the fish and other things that are only available with the salt."

"A seafood lover, are you? Not everyone likes certain delicacies of the sea."

Jane shrugged and didn't reply. Fred remembered that Carter had suspected the Cosburn sisters were from straightened circumstances. Some seafood was priced very cheap, which was why some of his acquaintances looked down upon it. He tried for a change of topic.

"Do you think we might have any acquaintances in common?" Fred was again chagrined by her uncomfortable response.

Jane's giggle sounded nervous as she shook her head. "Not likely, sir. Not that they would recall, in any case."

It was a rather odd response. "What do you mean by that?"

He watched in amazement as his wife took a deep breath and braced herself. Her face took on an almost apologetic expression, as though she were about to confess a great sin.

"I had to find employment."

Fred wasn't sure what she meant by that or how it related to his question, but from the expression on her face, he knew it was important that he try to understand what she wasn't saying.

"So, you were too busy to socialize? Is that what you're saying?"

He was relieved to note that while it might not have been the correct thing to ask, it also wasn't horribly wrong. She didn't appear to be any more uptight than she had, and perhaps he was merely being optimistic, but she might have even relaxed incrementally.

"That I very much was, yes," she replied with a small laugh. "But there is a possibility I might have been employed by some of your friends or acquaintances."

Fred waited for a beat, wondering if she would share any more information. When she didn't, he thought back to all that they had said. He had asked her if they might know any of the same people. Now, she was saying she might have worked for people he knew. And she was back to looking like she would rather the floor opened up and swallowed her. He felt at a loss and glanced toward Ella, who was trying to appear as though she weren't listening to their conversation. As such, she wasn't about to help him out.

Fred hoped he wasn't about to make a monumental mistake with his next words. "I have to say, Jane, with your looks, I strongly doubt any of my friends would have hired you and forgotten about you."

She stared at him for a moment, and her mouth actually fell open as though he had shocked her with his words. Her eyelashes fluttered for a moment, and then she burst into a fit of giggles.

"Are you jesting with me, sir?" she asked in between gasps for air as she struggled to gain control over her mirth.

"No, I'm not, and I will admit to you that I find your laughter confusing. It wasn't meant to be amusing."

This did nothing but send her deeper into the giggles. Finally, Fred joined her, although he had no idea what they were laughing about. Finally, after some moments, Jane propped herself fully upright in her chair, wiping the tears from her face with the edge of her sleeve, and beamed at him. She literally beamed. It was as though there were a glow around her, and Fred had to suck in his breath to control his physical reaction to her. How could this delicate creature be his wife? And how was he going to make her want to stay that way?

"Thank you so much, sir, I haven't laughed that hard in eons. It was just what I needed." She paused for a moment, bracing her shoulders. It appeared to Fred as though the laughter had leant her courage and she was about to divulge at least one of her secrets. He held his breath and thought a prayer for wisdom to say the right thing in response to whatever she might be about to reveal.

"You see, sir, I went into service when I was quite young. I have been a maid in many homes over the past several years. And in my experience, most of the well-to-do, if they are used to having servants, don't really notice them. So, while it is quite possible that I have cleaned your friends' homes, they most likely won't have noticed."

Fred blinked at her. He still wasn't sure what she was being so prickly about. But it was clearly apparent that she was sensitive about something that she had said. He rolled her words around in his mind. Quite young, been a maid, unnoticed. Which of those things was worse than the others?

"I'm sorry you had a tough time of things as a youngster. That can't have been easy. Hopefully now, in your new life with me, you will enjoy meeting my friends. But I hope you will tell me if there is anyone you don't wish to meet because you feel they have mistreated you."

Now it was her turn to blink at him. Her eyes filled with tears for the first time in their short acquaintance, and Fred wanted to rip out his tongue for saying the wrong thing to her.

Chapter Six

Jane's heart turned over, and so did her stomach. The man was too good to be true. No one had ever said something so solicitous to her in her life. At least, no man. Ella had been more than kind since Jane had come to stay, but Jane thought she was unique.

She hated to give way to tears, but she wasn't sure if she would be able to restrain the moisture that was gathering along her lashes. And the poor man looked aghast.

"I'm so sorry if I've offended you. I swear, I meant no offense. I think it's marvelous that you have done so well at looking after yourself. It's dreadful that you were forced to do so, but I'm impressed that you've managed to do so."

He was only making it worse, and Jane could tell he was getting desperate, but the more he said, the more her heart was pulled toward him. He was the loveliest man she had ever had the privilege to meet. And he was her husband! She would do all in her power to keep him. He must never know the rest of her background. Jane knew she had to pull herself together quickly or there'd be far more questions to face. So, she forced her lips into a smile.

"That is so very kind of you, sir. I promise you, I haven't been mistreated by any of my employers. It might be a little uncomfortable to socialize with them if they were to remember me, so it's just as well that I doubt they will."

"Then why did you nearly give way to tears?"

"Because no one has ever shown any concern about my feelings before?"

Jane was disconcerted by her husband's unwavering focus, even though she was certain he had heard Ella make a low sound of protest in the background. He ignored it, keeping his full attention on Jane. She felt as though she couldn't even blink. Jane forced her sluggish brain into action. She needed to distract him with a question of her own.

"I must ask, sir, why everyone calls you Fred. I thought your name was Alastair."

It did the trick. The man before her threw back his head and laughed. It was a sight to behold. His teeth were remarkably white, and she was certain he had all of them, a rarity in these parts to be sure, and not even so common in the city. His previously short-cropped hair had grown since he'd left Boston, and some of it slipped down over his eyebrow, giving him a boyish appearance. That, combined with the shine in his eyes as he gazed at her with laughter still dancing on his face, made her heart turn over. She didn't want to give her heart to her husband, but she was afraid it was going to happen without her say so. Jane quirked her eyebrow. The man's laughter was no true response to her question.

"I almost forget sometimes that my name is Alastair, to be honest with you. Everyone has been calling me Fred since I was a boy."

"But why? Fred Fredericksburg seems a little redundant, doesn't it?"

He laughed again but quieter this time. "I guess it does. But my sister, when she was young, had trouble learning to say certain sounds. Alastair was too much of a mouthful for her. So, she called me Fred, and it stuck so that everyone called me that."

"Did your mother not object?"

"She was too sick to notice when it first was happening, and then she died, so no, she didn't. And I don't think she would have minded," he quickly added. Jane thought he was trying to prevent an outpouring of sympathy from her. "She was just glad that Sybil and I were so close."

Jane swallowed her guilt with a gulp and nodded. "How old were you?"

"When Sybil was learning to speak? Or when we lost our mother?"

Jane shrugged and smiled a little. "Both, please." She enjoyed that he was sharing his story with her. Not that she wanted to do the same, but she would listen to him talk all day if he wished.

"I'm seven years older than Sybil. She was close to two when she was struggling with her speech. And I was ten when our mother died."

Jane's heart thumped hard in her chest. Something they had in common. Could it bind them or divide them?

"Me, too," she said.

He tilted his head in question. "You, too, for which part?"

Jane smiled. "I was ten when my mother died, too."

"I'm sorry. I think it's harder for girls to lose their mother than boys."

Jane shook her head. "I don't think any child should lose either parent. But it's life changing, that's for sure."

"At least ten is old enough to remember. Sybil doesn't have any memories of our mother. Mama was sick so much of Sybil's life, and then she was barely three years old when she died."

One more reason for Jane to feel sympathy for her new sister-in-law. She swallowed that down along with the rest and tried to keep a soft smile pinned to her face. Trying for lightness, Jane looked around and included Ella in her statement.

"It seems we're all orphans here, then, aren't we?" She quickly turned back toward Fred. "Or do you still have your father?"

"No, he died a few years ago. I'm an orphan, too," he concluded with a gentle smile toward her that made goose bumps prickle Jane's arms. He was lovely, and she wanted to keep him. What if he found out she wasn't a bargain?

"What sort of business do you do, sir?"

"Before I answer that, might I ask, why do you keep calling me, sir? Surely, we can be past a certain level of formality since we are married. I understand you might not be comfortable with me just yet as we've only met, but can you not call me by my name?"

Jane giggled, the sound a little nervous even to her own years. "The trouble is, I don't know what to call you. I'm inclined to use Alastair as that's your name, but your friends call you Fred, so I feel as though you'd want me to use that, but I didn't really know what was best."

"You could have asked," he reprimanded gently, making Jane feel heat climb in her cheeks. She hoped he would want to keep her, but she feared she wasn't doing a good job convincing him.

Hanging her head, she softly answered. "I'm sorry. What should I call you?"

Fred grasped her hand. "I'm sorry, too, I don't mean to scold you. We've just met. A lifetime of a certain etiquette is difficult to overcome, isn't it?" Jane hoped his question was rhetorical because she didn't really have a response for it. He continued. "A part of me wishes you *would* call me Alastair, but I'm afraid I might not respond to it."

This broke the awkward moment as they shared a chuckle.

"Very well, I'll use both at different times, in that case. It'll get you used to Alastair, perhaps. Or if you decide you don't like it, please, do tell me."

Jane was surprised when he reached out and grabbed her hand, shaking it. "It's a deal," he said.

Her heart had lodged itself in her throat. He lingered, holding her hand a moment before letting it go. It felt as though the heat from his warm palm had transferred itself to her own. It also seemed to suffuse her entire body. It was a pleasurable sensation.

Jane was always cold, probably because she always felt nervous. It was a welcome change to be suffused with heat. But knowing he was the source was disconcerting. It made her mind drift to matters she was uncomfortable contemplating, even though they were already legally wed.

She had just been given leave to use his first name, she doubted she should be thinking about sharing heat with the man. Just the thought made her heat up even more, and she knew her cheeks were flushing. At least she didn't feel faint, she thought as she remembered the mortifying experience when he had found her the day before.

"So, you didn't tell me what you do in Boston," Jane prompted, hoping to turn her thoughts.

Fred, or Alastair, smiled and her heart fluttered. She ignored it.

"I am a banker." He uttered the words with pride. "I haven't decided if I shall continue to work my job when we return to Boston, though. I recently acquired some investments that will provide sufficiently for our needs. And they might preoccupy too much of my time to allow me to keep the job."

Jane tilted her head, examining her husband's face. "You enjoyed your job, though, didn't you?"

"How can you know that?"

"Your face and voice give it away. What did you like about it? And will you be able to find those aspects in whatever else you might do?"

"You're right, I do enjoy my work at the bank. There are certain parts of it that I found highly stressful. I hate when we have to refuse someone a loan for something they truly want or need. Or when someone has spent all their money and didn't realize. Those instances were dreadful. But the interaction with many people was always a pleasure. And when we can say yes to a loan, especially if I know it's going to change their life for the better, that's the best feeling in the world. So, parts of that I'll be able to continue. I don't know if I'll be running into quite as many people, but perhaps I'll be able to take relationships deeper, which will be better anyway."

"That sounds delightful."

Jane could feel Fred's assessing gaze and tried to meet his eyes.

"You could help me, if you'd like."

She felt the blood leaving her face as she paled and suddenly felt light headed. Now she would have to tell him she hadn't any schooling. But then, she was saved unexpectedly.

Ella's sweet voice came from the kitchen. Jane rather thought they had both forgotten about her, as they started.

"I'm so sorry to have to interrupt your conversation, but I need to finish the meal set up."

Jane scrambled to her feet. "Let me help with that, Ella. I am so sorry that I have done nothing to help with the meal."

Ella rolled her eyes. "You have done plenty, my friend. But if you'd like, you could set the table and then help me carry the things. Fred, if you could go ring the bell on the porch, Carter will join us."

"That sounds fun," he answered with a grin.

Jane sighed as she watched him walk away. She doubted he could look bad if he tried, but especially when he smiled, it caused a flutter in his wake.

"You look like you're getting a little more comfortable with everything," Ella observed, a smile splitting her face.

Jane couldn't help but return the other woman's grin. But she still shrugged. "Comfortable might be too strong of a word, but I don't hate the idea. I still feel ridiculous for having run out on you all yesterday. But, yes, I'm much more settled with the idea of being Mrs. Fredericksburg."

"Even though it means going back to Boston?"

"I didn't hate it there like you did," Jane reminded her friend. Even though Jane had been a servant, she couldn't say her life had been bad. It had actually worsened here with her sister, since Phoebe's moods changed faster than the wind.

"So, we did a good thing marrying you off to Fred, then?"

Jane reached forward and clasped her friend's hands. "You did a truly lovely thing providing for me and keeping me safe from my sister and her strange plans of marrying me off to Avery Flynn. Did you know Fred was going to marry me himself when you wrote to him?" Jane hadn't thought to ask this when the news had arrived who her husband was.

Ella shook her head. "Not in the least. I thought he was a confirmed bachelor. You must remember, he's a fair bit older than his sister. She was the one I was such good friends with. So, from my childhood perspective, he was ancient. And since he had never married, he must've been far too old to do so at this point."

The two women laughed before Ella continued. "Of course, seeing him again, now, I realize he isn't so very old, just eight or so years older than me. The same age as Carter, I believe, and we only married recently. But, no, I can't say he crossed my mind as a possibility. Besides, with all the marriages he's arranged, he's had plenty of opportunities."

Jane frowned. "Makes me wonder why he decided to finally do it now."

Her stomach roiled. Why now? Why her? Did he think she had more going for her than she did?

"What if he's disappointed?" She didn't want to explain to her friend all her concerns, but she couldn't help voicing at least a little bit of her worries.

Ella reached out and clasped her hand. "You are a wonderful friend and a lovely young woman. You are a catch for any man, and don't you forget it." Her tone was scolding but was accompanied by a warm smile. "Besides, I don't know the details, but I understand your marriage helped him out, too, so don't you dare feel as though the favor is all one sided. He was lucky to get you, and you are going to do great wherever you go."

Jane squeezed her friend's hand and tried to return her smile with as much enthusiasm, but it was hard to muster. While a part of her longed to return to Boston, she feared the hierarchy that was Society there. She ought to have been welcomed there by her birth, but her circumstances had removed her far from that rarefied crowd. Now, Jane doubted she would see things in the same light as the others did. Would she be able to show a unified front with her husband?

Pushing the worries from her mind, Jane reminded herself that she was no longer that frightened servant girl. She was Jane Fredericksburg now, and she would be just fine. Her husband seemed inclined to look at their arrangement in a positive way. He wasn't examining her for her flaws. She would do her best to keep them all hidden, and they would be able to move along just fine.

The noon meal passed pleasantly, and while Jane didn't have too much to add to the conversation, she enjoyed witnessing Carter and Fred teasing and tormenting each other. Ella obviously had heard many of the stories they were referring to from her husband, so she was able to join in, but Jane didn't feel excluded even though it was all new to her. She could feel her husband's glances as though he were verifying to make sure she was fine. Finally, she smiled directly at him and leaned close.

"Stop worrying about me. I'm with friends here."

His eyes brightened, and he clasped her hand. This ended all chance of speech for Jane as her mind stuttered and her stomach fluttered. She could have sat there all day, watching the three friends and holding her husband's warm hand in her lap. But she didn't want him to think she was too clingy. Should she let go? Should she squeeze? Was it normal to wonder?

~ ~ ~

Fred enjoyed the attachment he felt to his new wife. He had been worried that she was feeling left out as he and Carter laughed about old events from their youth. Ella must have known the stories, as she was able to add her thoughts to their conversation, but Jane was new to all of it. It didn't seem to bother her, though.

He appreciated her serene smile and intelligent gaze as she watched the three of them enjoying themselves. He also appreciated the fact that she didn't want him worrying about her. Although that was his job now and he had every intention of doing it well.

The sensation of her small hand in his much larger one was sweet and comfortable. He had never thought he would be the type to want such an attachment, but from the moment he met her, Fred had felt an inclination to reach for Jane. It was disconcerting. But he didn't pull away. Until he could feel her begin to fret.

It was remarkable how attuned he had already become to her shifts in mood. It was as though the air around her vibrated. Carter and Ella didn't seem to notice, but Fred could tell she wasn't comfortable. Perhaps he was being too forward by holding her hand.

He tried to stifle his sigh as he let go and leaned back in his chair. For each bit of progress they made, he felt as though they also made a step backward. They needed to have a more thorough conversation.

"Thank you, for the delicious meal, Ella. I'm relieved to feel fully satisfied."

"For at least the next half hour, right?" Ella interrupted to tease him.

He didn't allow himself to be side-tracked. "Would you mind if Jane and I go for a walk? Perhaps she can show me a bit of your spread and we can discuss our plans."

"Sure, you two run along."

Jane protested slightly. "Oh, no, I ought to help you clean up."

Carter interrupted. "I don't have much planned for my afternoon. I'll help in here, Jane. We need to get used to not relying on you."

Fred felt badly for his wife. He knew Carter's words were meant to set her at ease, but Fred was fairly sure they hurt her feelings. He reached out and patted her shoulder once more, grateful that she didn't flinch away. She even sent him a weak smile.

"Shall we?" he asked as he pulled back her chair for her.

The blush that stained her cheeks was pretty, and his pulse thumped its appreciation. Fred fought to control it. He needed to have a serious discussion with his wife. He couldn't be distracted with her beauty or he'd be stuck in Missouri until they were wrinkled and grey.

Jane didn't say anything more but did precede him to the door. When they finally reached the porch, she turned to him with a half-smile. "Do you truly want to have a tour of the farm? Or were you just looking for a way to get out of the house?"

Chapter Seven

red wasn't sure how to answer her. She didn't appear to be afraid of his answer, but he was cautious anyhow. But he didn't want to lie to her either. Especially considering there were things he would prefer to keep from her for the time being.

"I will admit I've never been on a farm before, so I wouldn't mind seeing it a bit. While I am not so citified that I don't know that my food comes from farms, I pretty much never leave Boston, so I haven't had occasion to see any of the countryside. But I did hope we could have a little bit of privacy to discuss our plans."

He was pleased to see her nod and not run off. Her smile was a little strained, but she tucked her hand into the crook of his elbow.

"Come, see the chicks. They are the cutest thing you're likely to see right now. Many of the animals are pregnant. It seems to be a theme around here right now. But until the lambs and calves are born, the chicks are the closest you'll get to something cuddly. Unless you like mules."

Fred laughed. "Mules can be useful, but I've never considered them cuddly."

"Maggie the mule thinks she's a pet. Ella wanted pets when she arrived from Boston, so Carter let her baby any of the animals she wanted. She settled on Maggie as, again, there weren't any babies around at the time. Carter promised her a kitten from the first litter, but Maggie became Ella's pet. It's a rather amusing thing to watch the large mule looking for pats and treats."

"I'll take the chicks, first, then, please. I'll work my way up to Maggie."

Jane giggled but nodded sagely. "Wise choice."

They strolled away from the house toward a small barnlike structure near the shed where Fred had found apples earlier.

"Have you prepared yourself to move to Boston, Jane? I need to know if you think you'll be able to settle yourself into a new life."

She blinked at him with a puzzled frown. "I didn't really think there was a choice, sir." He must have frowned because she hurried to add, "I should say, Alastair." She smiled, even though it was a little thin, and continued. "I have no objection to moving back to Boston. I figured it was a given when the McLains sent my proxy to you. I would just as rather get away from my sister, anyway. I'm not sure if she's unwell in her mind or just mean, but I don't really wish to be her neighbor. So, there's nothing keeping me here except my friendship with Ella, and I have no desire to be beholden to her, however lovely she and Carter have been."

Fred was relieved to hear her say so. "Do you think we could set off sometime soon?"

She shrugged. Even though she looked a little nervous, she followed up with a nod. "I don't have much, so packing won't be an issue. I can be ready to go whenever you'd like."

Fred tried not to display his glee, but he must not have succeeded. Jane giggled. "Do you miss the city that much?"

Now it was Fred's turn to shrug. "I've already been gone for a week, and it will take at least five days to get back if there are no delays. So, while I wouldn't say I'm homesick, I am anxious to get back to my work."

Jane's wrinkled nose was so cute Fred caught his breath. But he kept his focus on the words that were forthcoming. "Most people would be glad for a holiday, I would think. I never minded being away from my work, except that we needed the money."

"Then you didn't have the right work, I would say."

Jane giggled. "I daresay. Maybe when we get to Boston, you can help me find a job that I won't want to be away from."

Fred stared at her in dismay. "Do you wish to work? I would rather you stay home. There is no need for you to work. You could involve yourself in charity work, if you'd like, but we certainly won't have any need for you to have an income."

He couldn't quite say what was flitting through her mind as a million emotions appeared to chase themselves around her face. She giggled again, but it sounded forced.

"I'll look forward to learning all about our new life in Boston, then."

Fred had to be satisfied with that. On the surface, it was exactly what he wanted. But he was left with the feeling that there was something he was missing. With a mental shrug, he decided they had the rest of their lives to figure it out. And at least five days on the train to discuss things.

"Do you think tomorrow might be too soon?" he asked tentatively.

The expression on her face looked equal parts trepidation and bravery. "There's really little to gain by staying here. We're married now, and as far as I understand, there's no changing that. The McLains vouch for my safety with you, and I trust them. We can get to know one another as easily or as awkwardly on the train as here, I suppose. Perhaps being with a bunch of strangers on the train will actually be less awkward."

Fred laughed. "You've got a point there."

Jane blinked for a moment as though she were surprised at the turn of events, even though she agreed to it. She then nodded firmly and offered him a small smile.

"Well then, if this is to be your only day here, you really ought to see it all."

Fred was unsure about the wisdom of her words. His mixed feelings must've been written all over his face because she laughed and offered to let him off the hook.

"Of course, since you haven't seen your friends in years, you might rather spend some time with them, since you'll have plenty of time with me in the coming days."

Now he worried he would sound churlish either way. But he tried to say the right thing. "I've been enjoying your company thus far. But you do have a point about Carter. Perhaps you could show me this friendly mule, and then I'll return to see what Carter is up to."

Jane laughed. Her amusement and previous description of the animal made Fred nervous, but he was relieved when they arrived near its fence that it only snuffled around his pockets. He had experience with horses, so he knew quite well what she was after, but he had not come prepared.

"Aww, poor Maggie will be disappointed if we don't have anything for her," Jane commented before producing a couple chunks of cut apples from her pocket.

Fred lifted his eyebrows and grinned at her. "Did you learn from your long walk to never leave home without apples?"

Jane joined him in amusement. "That was an aberration for me, to be honest. I almost always have something in my pockets, since I enjoy walking amongst the animals. They are far more welcoming if you don't come empty handed. Especially Maggie, here."

The animal seemed to recognize her name and the teasing she was receiving. Her ears swiveled, and she tossed her head but took the pieces of apple gently from Jane's hand before butting her head into the young woman's chest. Fred reached out to steady her, but she just laughed and shook her head.

"That's just Maggie's way of showing affection. Like I said, she thinks she's a pet. I think she'd rather be a kitten or a lapdog."

Fred grinned. "She's a little large for that."

Jane shushed him. "Don't tell her that, it'll hurt her feelings." And the daft woman actually patted the animal's head, scratching her ears, and crooning as though to comfort the large animal. Fred's skepticism must've danced across his face because, as they walked away, Jane giggled softly.

"Don't worry, Alastair, I swear I'm not daft. And I promise not to ask for a mule as a pet when we return to the city."

"Well that's a relief." His reply was too enthusiastic. Jane burst into laughter.

"Were you seriously worried?"

"Of course, not," he replied, but she didn't appear convinced. Fred hurried to continue the conversation along as they strolled toward the house.

"You appear to like animals, but I haven't seen you with a pet of your own. Will there be any critters accompanying us on the train?"

Now it was Jane's turn to raise skeptical eyebrows toward him. "That sounds highly uncomfortable for all parties, wouldn't you think?"

Fred shrugged. "I would try to work it out for you, if you did."

"That's kind of you, thank you, but no, I don't have any pets. I have actually never had a pet. I was deemed too young before my mother died and then had too many responsibilities afterward. Then I felt it would be cruel to a pet if I was never home to care for it. And since I've been out here, I just never found the right time. It wasn't perfectly comfortable at my sister's and here with the McLains, there are plenty of animals and it was a temporary situation at best. So again, not the time for a pet."

"Will you want one when we get home?"

Jane smiled at him, and Fred could have sworn there were tears in her eyes. He wanted to question her but didn't want to embarrass her. He couldn't imagine what he might have said to make her cry.

"I will think about it, thank you."

Fred hadn't meant to offer her carte blanche for animals, but he didn't bother arguing the point. Hopefully she would raise the subject again before coming home with any animals.

~~~

Jane struggled for composure as she walked at her husband's side. She had a husband! And he spoke of home. Jane hadn't truly felt at home since losing her mother. She hadn't even realized how much she was longing for a home until he mentioned it. Now, she couldn't wait. But she tried to rein in her anticipation. She couldn't be sure his home would feel like home to her until she got there and spent some time in it. And of course, he couldn't have any idea how enticing this word would be for her. But it was clear he didn't intend for her to feel uncomfortable in his home. He was offering his life to her. And she had every intention of grasping it with both hands and holding on tight.
~~~

She wracked her brain trying to think of something else to discuss on the short walk back to the house.

"Do you have much family in Boston? You've mentioned your sister, Sybil. Do you have more siblings? You don't have any parents, but what about extended family?" Jane didn't particularly wish to discuss Sybil, but it would probably be unnatural not to ask about family. Not that she really wanted to talk about her own family, either. On second thought, it was a rather daft conversational turn, she rebuked herself.

Fred saved her from too much discomfort when he answered her.

"Actually, I have very little family. No other siblings, and you know we lost our mother when we were young, something you and I have in common. Our father also passed away a few years ago. There are a few cousins, but we are a small family." He paused for a moment, casting her a sideways glance. "I wouldn't mind to change that, though."

It took her a moment to discern his meaning. She then felt as though her entire body were consumed with the heat of her blush. "Oh, well, yes, of course..." She began to stammer out a reply. "I would love to have children one day," she added shyly after a deep breath helped to stem the tide of her stuttering.

He again saved her from prolonged discomfort by asking her the same question. "What about you? Do you have any family still in Boston?"

"Not really," she answered. It wasn't completely untrue. She didn't consider any of those people to be her family. To her way of thinking, family didn't mistreat one another. Jane wondered if she would have to encounter them. She should try to ask Ella how extensive were Alastair's social connections. Jane had never told Ella her full story, but Jane well knew about Ella's social past, so she knew the other woman would understand the question and should know the answer.

She was saved from any further explanation despite Alastair's quizzical expression, as they had arrived back on the porch and Carter was just exiting the house.

"Fred, my boy, has Jane showed you everything there is to see?"

"Uh, not everything, I don't think."

"Good. Come, let's saddle up and I'll brag up my property to you. My wife is convinced you'll be leaving us shortly, so I want to take some time to show you how I've done for myself."

Jane watched as they walked toward the barn, amused as Alastair glanced back toward her. His expression seemed to ask her to save him, but there was nothing she could do to intervene. And they had agreed he would spend the last bit of time here with his friend.

Jane shook her head. The man truly was citified. She didn't mind, really. Having experienced both, she would say she would prefer the city, too, if they had the means. From what she could tell, being poor was more comfortable in the country than the city. For one thing, you could grow your own food. And it was less obvious who had less or more.

From what she could tell of her husband, he wasn't poor. And he didn't appear to have any intention of sending her off to work. So, she would happily accompany him back to Boston. She could barely remember life in the city before it became so difficult. Jane was looking forward to reacquainting herself with the other side of the city.

The afternoon and evening flew by. Ella insisted on sending a couple of her fancier frocks back to Boston with Jane.

"I haven't any need for such things here, Jane, and well you know it. I can't even tell you what Sybil was thinking when she sent them to me. I've worn each of them once, just to say that I did. You and I are of a similar size. You can easily get away with wearing them without even doing any alterations. It'll get you started until you can get some things of your own."

Jane had wanted to weep over her friend's generosity. And though she wanted to refuse the other woman's charity, she recognized the truthfulness of her words. There really was nowhere to wear clothes that were impractical here on Carter's spread. Jane knew Ella had plenty of gowns; she wouldn't miss the two she was giving Jane. She tried to be gracious in her acceptance. And she knew she would be grateful once she arrived in Boston. The few items of clothing she owned would be unacceptable in her role as a banker's wife.

Even with the two extra gowns, it took no time to have her things packed. Jane kept herself busy helping Ella prepare the meal and do any final cleaning Jane could think of. Ella had tried to stop her, but Jane had explained herself.

"For one thing, I'm a little too anxious about tomorrow to sit still and sip tea. And for another, I'm just so very grateful to you and your husband for taking me in for the last few weeks."

"Jane Cosburn, you've earned your keep thrice over with all the help you've been to me since you've been here. I never would have gotten so many baby things prepared without your help, and there's no way the house would be this spotlessly clean if I had been on my own."

Jane laughed at her scolding tone. "Well, it was the least I could do. And now you've arranged this new life for me. I really have no way of repaying you."

Ella's face softened. "Be a good, kind wife to our friend, and we'll be more than even."

Jane choked on her words. "I'll do my very best."

Ella clasped her hand. "I know you will, my friend. But I also know you're terrified. What can I do to help?"

And they spent the rest of the afternoon gossiping and giggling as they finished the supper preparations. As soon as the meal had been consumed, Jane excused herself. She wasn't sure if she would be able to sleep, but she couldn't bear to sit and agonize over the next day. And she was sure Alastair would enjoy one last visit with his friends.

Much to her surprise, she drifted right off to sleep. Perhaps it was still the effects of her exertions the day before, or perhaps her body was comforted by the presence of hope in her heart. Whatever the case, she awoke to the birds and a bright sun, rested and anticipating her new future. If there was a little fly in the ointment preventing her from pure joy, she chose to ignore that niggling fact.

75

Chapter Eight

Fred was uncomfortable as they waited for the train. Carter and Ella had offered to wait with them, but it was going to be another hour, and since they had already done all their talking, it would have been awkward for all of them as they made idle chatter and waited with the small group of people awaiting the next train.

The size of the group heading east was a surprise. Fred would have thought he and Jane would be the only ones heading east. Since it was spring, most were going in the opposite direction to try their luck in the great expanse. With no trains going west that day, he would have thought they would have the station to themselves, but there were a few others milling around.

Jane had shed tears over her goodbyes to the McLains. Fred had wondered how to comfort her but other than patting her on the shoulder as Ella and Carter drove away, he wasn't sure what he could do. They still were strangers, after all. He wondered if he ought to ask about her sister. But then he realized he didn't want to bring up such a potentially painful subject when the poor woman was already feeling sensitive.

He needn't have worried. She turned toward him, her eyes luminous after her weeping. Fred was relieved her tears seemed to have dried. But then more welled up as she started to speak.

"I had secretly thought Phoebe would have come to send us off. Or that she would have come by Carter's, even though he told her to stay away. Under the circumstances, I'm sure he would have allowed it. He had one of the men go by and tell them we were leaving, so I know she is aware."

Fred took a deep breath and prayed for the right words. "It's possible she realized how dreadful goodbyes are and didn't want to subject you to hers."

This produced a watery chuckle from his wife and chased away her tears. "That's diplomatic of you, Alastair. Thank you. Yes, you're right, it is possible those were her thoughts. Not probable, but possible." She laughed again. "Anyhow, have you traveled by train often? I know you mentioned you don't like to leave the city, but I was wondering if you're as inexperienced as me."

"I don't leave the city frequently, but I have ridden the train between Boston and New York a number of times."

Jane nodded. "I would think that would be a frequently used train line."

Fred smiled. "Are you feeling nervous or uncertain about our mode of travel?"

Jane shrugged. "Not particularly anxious, but I am curious about its reliability. Are we likely to be waiting long, do you suppose? Or is it expected to arrive at the time they said?"

Fred nodded in understanding over her questions. "Since this particular line doesn't start too very far from here, it's unlikely there would be many delays between its start and here. It's entirely possible that we won't arrive in Boston at the predicted time as it is a long way, and any number of things could hold us up, but I don't expect we'll be kept waiting here too much longer."

He was pleased to see a sunny smile grace his wife's face. "That's a relief. I find once I get going, I'm much more settled about things. Right now, the anticipation is making me a little anxious."

"Was your ride out here your first time on the train?"

"Yes, and it wasn't the most comfortable experience. I expect the return trip will be much better."

"Why is that?"

"For one thing, it seems you paid more than I did, so I'm expecting the accommodations to be better. And I won't be a single woman alone traveling west."

"Ah, I see. I can imagine that might not have been the most comfortable situation to be in. Were you put in some awkward positions?"

Jane laughed. "It depends if you consider multiple propositions to be awkward. Some were legitimate propositions of marriage, some less so. None of them were acceptable."

Fred was curious, since she had ended up wedding a stranger. "What made them so unacceptable?"

"Did Carter not tell you that one of my requirements in a groom was that he have at least some teeth and knew his way to the cleansing bowl?"

Fred threw back his head and laughed. "As I recall, he did mention teeth and cleanliness as requirements. I thought he was funning me."

"You thought it funny that was a requirement?"

"No! I thought those things were a given. Carter also mentioned economic stability and health. I took those seriously. But, yes, I thought he was teasing about the teeth, as I would never consider someone who couldn't keep up with basic hygiene."

Jane's sunny smile returned. "So, that is how I found myself arriving in Council Bluff without a groom."

Fred grinned along with her. "Such a sad state of affairs when one sets their standards so high."

She imitated his fake serious tone. "Yes, I have tried to curb my overachieving expectations, but what can one do when one was raised in the elevated Society of Boston?"

"One must return there with haste. That is what one must do."

Jane laughed again. "Exactly."

Her ready sense of humor pleased him. Basically, everything about her pleased him. But it made him a little nervous. He didn't know her well enough, and she wasn't showing any signs of giving her heart to him. Fred certainly didn't want to fall in love with his wife before he had made her fall in love with him. He would have to make sure that happened. If he had bound her to himself both legally and emotionally, maybe then he could trust her with all the details of their marriage.

Before he could set his plan in motion, their train arrived. As he had predicted, it was within ten minutes of the posted arrival time. That slight delay would likely grow over the coming days. He tried to tell himself not to expect their arrival to be quicker than a week. Then he wouldn't be too disappointed if it turned out to be true.

He was pleased to see the accommodations weren't as sparse as he had found them to be on his ride west until he realized they were exactly the same.

"What are you laughing about?" Jane's tone held curiosity and perhaps a dose of speculation that he wasn't as sound mentally as she had expected.

"I was just thinking how spacious the room is. It's amazing how your perspective can change so quickly."

She still looked puzzled.

"While I was travelling west, I had thought the accommodations on the train were cramped and Spartan. But after a few nights in the bunkhouse, I can appreciate this room as luxurious. We don't even have to share it with anyone."

"Except each other," she reminded him.

"Is that so very dreadful if I promise to keep to my side of the room?"

She blushed and shook her head. "Thank you, Alastair. I know you're being remarkably patient with me."

"I completely understand that we are still strangers. Don't let it trouble you. Hopefully, before long we'll be old friends as well as husband and wife."

He was amused by her deepening blush but had mercy on her, offering a change of scenery. "You must be hungry since breakfast has now been hours ago."

Her shy nod prompted a chuckle out of him but he simply said, "Let's go find the dining car and put an end to our stomachs' grumbling."

This finally put her at ease, and she joined him in laughter as they made their way down the narrow hallway. She had to skim her hand along the wall to maintain her balance, but otherwise seemed to be adjusting well to the motion of the train.

"You are quite adaptable for a young woman from the city."

She tilted her head like an inquisitive bird, watching him with her intelligent gaze but not replying to his comment.

"You don't even seem to be bothered by the motion of the train. You seemed perfectly comfortable on McLain's property, but you also seem to be taking your return to the city in stride."

They were interrupted by the waiter taking their order, but when they returned their attention to each other, she was smiling at him. Jane shook her head.

"I have had to adjust to drastically different circumstances a few times in my life. I wouldn't say I've gotten used to it, but since the first big change happened when I was still quite young, perhaps it has made me resilient. But it has also put me in a habit of not getting too attached. That may not be healthy within a relationship."

Fred raised his eyebrows at her. "Do you wish to become attached to me?" He was pleased that she was thinking that way.

She shrugged. "It would probably be helpful to a successful marriage, wouldn't you think? Ella certainly seems attached to Carter."

"Is your sister attached to her husband?"

"That just proves my point. No, she's not. And they don't seem to be at all happy. I certainly don't want to emulate them."

Fred nodded. "I can see your point," he said, although, thinking of his sister and her attachment to her louse of a husband, he wasn't sure how he felt on the subject. "Sybil and Horace seem to swing between extremes. On occasion, Horace will shower her with attention and even gifts, and Sybil seems to thrive. But more often than not, he is cold and aloof toward her. He feels as though she entrapped him into their marriage and resents her for it. They married rather suddenly. Although Sybil had been hoping he would come up to scratch, Horace had seemed reluctant to commit. And then, all of a sudden, he proposed marriage, and they were married within weeks. To be honest with you, I had been expecting there would quickly be a child. I shouldn't have listened to the gossips."

Jane suddenly seemed very uncomfortable with the subject, so he pushed thoughts of Sybil from his mind and enjoyed his wife's company.

He tried to get to know her over the next few days but it was, at times, difficult. Some of his questions seemed to fluster or embarrass her. Fred didn't know why she would be uncomfortable telling him her favorite books or what she enjoyed doing to pass the time. Finally, he settled for telling her about himself. Strangely, that seemed to please her and set her at ease.

"Carter didn't enjoy school. It was surprising when you consider how good a student he was. Or maybe it was just that he was a quick learner. He always did well on examinations. But he hated the constraints of school life."

"And you didn't?"

Fred enjoyed her intelligent gaze and probing questions. He smiled at her.

"Not like he did. Our friend Ransom was the same. We were boys together, growing up in the same neighborhood and then continuing on to University. Ransom managed to graduate before he went west, but Carter only lasted about a year with us before he took off to the wilds."

She was gazing at him like an inquisitive bird again, with her head cocked to the side, studying him carefully.

"I can't tell if you're wistful about him leaving you, or that you didn't go with either of them."

Fred laughed. "I can assure you, I have no aspirations for life in the wild western portions of our great country. I'm glad that I've seen it for myself now, but I'm all the more convinced that the city life is for me."

He was glad when she nodded, as though in agreement.

"Tell me more about University. What did you love learning the most?"

Fred was pleased to comply, and the time flew by pleasantly.

Chapter Nine

Jane could hardly believe it. The days had flown by, and now they were about to pull into the station at their final destination. They hadn't even been delayed too much along the way. Alastair was nearly giddy with delight that it had only taken them six days. Not even, if you considered the fact that they were arriving fairly early in the morning, whereas they had left in the afternoon.

Jane stifled her yawn behind her hand. She hadn't slept well since they left Carter and Ella's home. She wasn't sure if it was the constant motion of the train or her discomfort being alone with her husband, but she was looking forward to sleeping in a solid bed that night. And if she could manage it, she would love to catch a nap, too. Napping was the most decadent activity she had yet encountered. It wasn't something she had done since childhood, but it had become a habit of theirs over the past days. There wasn't that much to do on the train, and neither of them had slept soundly.

Perhaps it was the constant awareness of the other. Or maybe that was just her. It felt to Jane as though she could feel him breathing. That his very presence vibrated around her. He had been very kind about allowing her privacy and not forcing his attentions upon her. It had been an awkward conversation, but she had appreciated it none the less.

His uncomfortable throat clearing had alerted her to the upcoming difficult conversation. Jane had noticed that Alistair did that whenever he was nervous. It had been their first evening on the train.

"Since we have a rather unconventional arrangement, I thought we ought to discuss the state of our marriage."

Jane's stomach had clenched. Was he about to say that he was going to abandon her as soon as they reached Boston?

"What did you have in mind?" She kept her tone as neutral as possible, not revealing her own feelings, grateful that the high neck of her gown would hide the fact that her pulse had accelerated at an alarming rate.

"I thought you might be apprehensive about the intimacies of marriage."

Jane had to giggle. "You thought correctly."

She watched in fascination as his cheekbones darkened. He cleared his throat once more. "Has anyone explained these matters to you?"

Now, Jane's face was flaming. She shook her head.

Alastair cleared his throat yet again. "Yes, of course not. I forgot you've lost your mother. And of course, your sister wouldn't have explained. I thought perhaps Ella would have, but never mind about that. I will explain it to you later." The poor man tugged on his cravat and looked as though he wished he had never started this conversation. "I thought perhaps you would prefer if we set a parameter to our relationship. Like, we'll consider intimacies in a month's time, once we've come to know one another."

Jane nearly sagged in relief. The fact that he didn't seem to have any intention of abandoning her, added to the reprieve on needing to explore the mysteries of the marital bed, was almost too good to be true. She blinked at him, surprised by the offer. Now it was her turn to clear her throat as it clogged with sudden emotion.

"That might be best," was all she could muster to say.

"Do you think a month will be enough time for you?"

His tone sounded funny to Jane's ears. She examined his face, wondering why he couldn't quite meet her gaze. What was he hiding? She tried to question him but started with a shrug.

"Since I've never been married, nor intimate, I really have no way of knowing, to be frank. But it seems reasonable."

Alastair nodded, his cheeks darkening once more. "The thing is, I find you remarkably attractive and don't think it's reasonable to expect me to wait longer, but I don't want to rush you into something you wouldn't be ready for."

Jane now understood his shifty gaze, as she could no longer look him in the face either. But she did her best to nod and respond. "I appreciate your honesty and your consideration. I'm sure it'll be better for us once we have gotten to know one another."

From the corner of her eye she saw him nodding. "Shall we start now?"

Her gaze flew to his. "Start what?"

Alastair chuckled. "Start getting to know one another," he explained through his laughter. "I know very little about you. Your full name and date of birth were on the documents Carter sent for our marriage, but that's about it. There's so much more I ought to know. And you should know things about me, too, I suppose."

Jane felt her eyes widen. It was true. She wanted to know everything about him. But she didn't want him to know everything about her. Which made her a hypocrite. What to do?

She forced a yawn. "It has been a rather intense few days and I'm quite tired. Do you think we could start on the story telling in the morning?"

The smile he gave her was equal parts kindness and understanding with perhaps a little bit of relief added in. Jane wondered if he, too, had things he would rather leave unsaid. For a moment, she regretted putting it off but decided her own urge for self-preservation would exceed her desire for knowledge about him for now.

"Very well. I will step out for a few minutes to allow you to ready yourself for sleep."

Jane appreciated his absence and his return. She wouldn't have wanted to change in front of him but was nervous on her own. This trip was going to be a far cry from her journey west where she had only purchased a seat and didn't change her clothes for the entire week.

It was still difficult to sleep once he returned, but being on a berth rather than a seat made it somewhat possible. Jane found her ears attuned to his every shift or movement. That subsided slightly as the days passed, but only a very little. If anything, as she got to know him, a certain awareness increased. If his hand drew near enough to touch her, she was torn between a desire to flinch away and an urge to get closer.

~ ~ ~

The last week had been torture. Pleasurable torture. But torture none the less. Fred had lain in the berth across from his wife listening to her steady breathing night after night. He was almost certain she wasn't sleeping any better than he was, but she hid it better than he did. He didn't want to complain. He was enjoying getting to know her.

Jane seemed to be a sweet, young woman with a steady demeanor. His first impression of her after she had run away when she knew he was to arrive had not been truthful. It was becoming clear to him that her reaction then was not really in keeping with her character. She wasn't flighty or impulsive. If anything, she thought everything through for an excruciating length of time. Whenever he asked her a question, she had paused to ponder before answering.

Like when he had asked her about when she had started working. "How old were you when you found your first employment?" He had thought it an innocuous question. But it felt like ten minutes passed before she answered him. Perhaps he was exaggerating, but he had actually had to check to see if she had fallen asleep. And she never did fully answer his question.

"It was about a month after my mother died," she finally said in a soft voice. Her tone was almost dreamy, as though her thoughts were elsewhere, but when he peered closer, he could see that there were tears glistening in the corners of her eyes, so he didn't want to pry deeper.

"I think you were quite young, then, weren't you?" he had still felt inclined to ask.

"In my opinion, any time is too young to lose your mother, wouldn't you agree?" Her question, and the wistful tone, had brought a lump to his own throat as he remembered losing his mother, and especially how that loss had affected Sybil, his young sister.

"Yes, you're quite right," he had finally answered. They then both found themselves staring off into space.

But Fred hadn't wanted to give up completely. A few minutes later, he cleared his throat and asked some more questions. He didn't really think she was trying to avoid telling him about herself, but that was how it was turning out.

"Did you enjoy the work you found?"

This time she finally faced him, but the expression on her face was one of profound sadness, making him wish he hadn't asked.

"I would have preferred being with my friends," she answered softly. "But my father needed help supporting the family."

"Did your brothers and sisters also find work?"

She shook her head but didn't say anything else. Fred was growing uncomfortable, so he launched into his own tale.

"I was only fifteen when I got my first job," he could hear pride in his voice. "I juggled school and work for years."

"How did you manage that?" she had asked.

Fred felt his chest puffing with pride over the admiration he could hear in her voice. The memory of that conversation still brought a smile to his face. His pretty little bride looked up to him. It was the most intoxicating sensation he could ever remember feeling.

Fred glanced over at the dainty creature who was his wife and couldn't help smiling over the small frown between her brows. She was a worrier, and he found it endearing. Fred enjoyed it when she finally unburdened herself to him. It wasn't often, but as the week had progressed, there had been a few times that she had expressed herself. Before she had done so, she had the very same frown between her brows. He was both relieved and happy when the frown had smoothed out after they had discussed whatever had been concerning her.

The first time had been about money. It was their first morning on the train. It had become obvious that she was putting off leaving their room, but he couldn't imagine why. Fred, himself, was becoming ravenously hungry, and still she was putting off leaving. That frown had become more deeply embedded in her forehead.

Finally, with a touch of exasperation, he had asked her point blank. "Is there a reason you wish to remain in this small room?"

Color had ebbed and flowed on her face, but she had finally faced him. "I don't have any money."

Fred had blinked at her in surprise, unsure what to make of her statement. "What do you mean?" he had thought to ask, hoping she would explain her thoughts more clearly.

"I gave all my earnings to Phoebe when I arrived in Trader's Bluff and continued to do so after my arrival. She said she was keeping it safe for me. But when she kicked me out, she said I had forfeited it. She gave over a little bit to Carter when he went to speak to Phoebe's husband, but I spent that on my ticket."

As tears welled in her eyes, Fred's heart clenched. He hated to feel attracted to her sadness, but she looked beautiful as she gazed up at him as though beseeching him. Distracted by her beauty, it took his brain a few beats to catch up to what she was saying.

"Do you want me to give you some money? Are you feeling uncomfortable without your own funds?"

"No, I don't want you to give me money. Money needs to be earned. I just don't have any, so I cannot buy anything."

Again, Fred was left blinking at her without comprehension. "You are my wife. What's mine is yours. That is how this works. Would you begrudge me your money, if you had it?"

Her frown was back, but it appeared to be one of puzzlement rather than worry. "No, I wouldn't begrudge you anything." Her breathy tone was once again a distraction, but Fred tried to maintain his focus to get to the bottom of his wife's concerns.

"So, you will allow me to buy you some breakfast, right?"

She opened her mouth as though to object, but then she met his gaze and her face creased into a small smile. "Thank you, Alastair, I would enjoy sharing breakfast with you."

Fred felt his chest puffing up, again, over her use of his formal name as well as her gentle smile. He felt like a king as he had solved one small problem for his pretty, young wife. As they made their way to the dining car, he couldn't help patting her hand where it lay on his elbow, even though it was awkward walking together in the tight quarters. He couldn't bear to be separated from her. Which did not bode well for his return to work upon their arrival in Boston, he thought with a slight jolt.

"Have you given any more thought to what you would like to do with your time once we get home?" Fred asked after they had placed their orders.

It wasn't the right question, as it brought a small frown back to her face, but she didn't appear as though she were overly upset. It did take her a while to answer his question, though, but the wait was worth it.

"I would like to be occupied. It isn't likely that we'll have children to be concerned with for at least a year, so I should find something noble to do with my time. I liked your suggestion of doing some charitable works. I know there are many young women who find themselves in unwelcome circumstances through no fault of their own. If they don't have family to turn to and illness or injury prevents them from working, they can pretty quickly get in a bad way. I'm sure there must be something that can be done for them, even if it is as simple as providing a meal or some clean clothes."

"That sounds like a worthy cause. I'm sure the wives of some of my friends or business associates might also like to join you. Or perhaps they already have something in place that you could help with."

Her smile that had been so brilliant when he praised her idea had dimmed a little when he mentioned his acquaintances, but Fred didn't allow that to discourage him. He was glad she had actually thought about the matter. He knew she was used to working and didn't want her to be bored while he was tied up with business. He was also gratified that she mentioned children. He would enjoy seeing her round with his child one day. Again, he could feel his chest swelling. Fred stifled his amusement. He was going to become a strutting peacock before long.

And so, the days passed. Fred wouldn't have been able to say what all he learned about his wife in specific detail, but he certainly could say that his heart beat faster whenever his eyes landed on her pretty face. If she could ever bring herself to start a conversation with him, he nearly became lightheaded. Which was truly ridiculous, he chided himself. She was just a young woman. He needn't turn into a ninny over her. But she was his wife, so he supposed it wasn't so very farfetched that he ought to develop feelings for her. He just hoped she was doing the same for him. He didn't want to ask, but he knew it would be dreadful if these feelings were not reciprocated.

~ ~ ~

Stepping down onto the platform, Jane knew it was her sister-in-law waiting for them, even before she heard Alastair calling out for her.

"Sybil, my dear, I didn't expect to find you waiting for us," he exclaimed as he pulled her into a warm embrace.

Jane tried not to be jealous. The other woman was his sister. Jane ought to be happy to see her husband comfortably displaying his affection. Perhaps one day, he would do the same for her. But she wholeheartedly wished he would do so now. Besides the fact that she had absolutely no desire to face her new sister-in-law. But she bolstered her courage and pasted as realistic a smile as she could muster upon her face as she stepped forward to be introduced to her husband's only relative. Searching the other woman's face, Jane was thrilled not to see a drop of recognition. This led her smile to grow in warmth.

"It's a pleasure to meet you, Sybil. Your brother has told me so much about you."

"He has, has he?" Sybil asked with a light laugh. "Don't believe everything he tells you. I wasn't nearly so dreadful as he likes to describe."

Jane laughed, too, and it almost sounded genuine to her ears. "He hasn't said anything dreadful, I promise. It's obvious to me the two of you are very close."

Sybil smiled softly. "I owe him everything."

Now Fred looked uncomfortable. "The good and the bad," he added.

Jane wanted to question what he meant, but the look the siblings exchanged made her feel that she would be intruding if she asked any questions. So, she merely smiled at them and waited for Alastair to take the lead.

"I didn't think you would be here. You didn't have to come. We could have dropped by your house later."

Sybil swatted her brother's arm playfully. "I know you, my darling brother. You will be off to your office before your wife has even looked around your house. I didn't think you would be able to bear to come for a visit after two weeks away."

Alastair cast her a guilty face but didn't deny her words.

"See what I mean," Sybil said to Jane as she put her arm through her elbow. Jane was acutely uncomfortable but couldn't reject the friendly overture. "I've been wanting a sister since I was old enough to understand what that meant. Unfortunately, our mother died before she could fulfill my wish. I'm thrilled that Fred has, once again, given me exactly what I wanted. So, no, Fred darling, I couldn't sit at home in the hopes that you would drop by. I have been haunting the train station to get updates on arrivals. I will not be denied my new sister for another minute."

Jane quelled the guilty feelings that were threatening. Surely, the woman wouldn't be nearly so vivacious if she had been leading a dreadful life, she assured herself. Turning to meet her husband's gaze, she couldn't interpret the thoughts crossing his face.

"I had thought to have my wife to myself as I showed her our home, Sybil." His tone was mild, but Jane felt heat climbing her cheeks at what he was implying. Thankfully, his sister didn't seem to care.

"No, you didn't, Fred, and don't you try to bamboozle me. You're thrilled I'm here. You can't tell me you've changed into a new person in two weeks, even if you have acquired a wife. And I dare say, you don't even know where your linen closets are or anything useful about your house, since I helped you pick it out. I'll show Jane her new home, and you can run and make sure your office is still where you left it, then we can all be perfectly comfortable."

"Horace won't mind?" Alastair's gentle question caused a flicker of disquiet to cross her face, making Jane's heart sink, but Sybil quickly rallied.

"He might not even notice, to be honest. I promise not to overstay, but you cannot begrudge me this. You have been gone for two weeks. I need some sibling time." She did a little dance as they walked toward a row of carriages that appeared to be for hire. "I'm just that excited to now have two siblings."

Jane couldn't help but join in the other woman's enthusiasm. She had never been on the receiving end of such an exuberant welcome and couldn't find it in herself to quell her sister-in-law's excitement. It seemed Alastair couldn't deny his sister either.

"Very well, minx, perhaps you are right. You'll be better suited to show Jane the house than I would be."

Jane refused to allow herself to be disappointed. She did want to be friends with Sybil. And since she and Alastair were still getting to know one another, it might be less awkward to be with someone else when they first entered their house. The silence of two people in a house might be deafening. Not that they had been having trouble with conversation.

That was one of the things she had most enjoyed about their time on the train. They had hours to talk and visit with one another. She rather thought she knew everything there was to know about him. Fact-wise, anyhow. Jane was still certain her husband was holding something back from her, but she hadn't a clue what it could possibly be. Perhaps he, too, had a secret about her or a family member. Wouldn't that be delicious irony?

Alastair arranged for a hired carriage to drive them home and stowed their luggage all the while Sybil was chattering about Boston happenings.

"And there's to be a fund-raising ball at the end of the week, surely you must present, Jane, Fred." Sybil turned to Jane with typical enthusiasm. "You will love Mrs. Truman's balls, Jane. She always has the most organized fund raisers."

"Which cause is she supporting now?" Alastair's tone was bored, much to Jane's surprise.

Her thought must have been written upon her face. She was surprised that he noticed.

He explained himself quietly. "Mrs. Truman loves to be the center of attention. Her balls and fund raising efforts, while of course, for good causes, are, in my opinion, just a reason for her to throw some sort of grand affair that her husband will not object to."

Jane blinked. "Why would she do that?"

"So we all think she is worthy and noble."

"Perhaps she *is* worthy and noble," Jane pointed out, puzzled.

"You'll see," was all Alastair would say.

"Never mind him, Jane, he doesn't really like the Trumans. But her balls are divine. Will your luggage arrive in time? If you don't have a proper ball gown, we could go shopping tomorrow or you could borrow something of mine. You don't look too much taller than me and while you're thinner, that's easy enough to adjust."

Jane didn't know how to react to Sybil's comments and didn't want to commit herself to anything until she had a chance to discuss it with her husband. She had no real desire to socialize at a fund raiser, and it didn't seem like he wanted to go, besides the fact that she had no intention of asking her husband to buy her a ball gown. If they did attend, she would be happy enough to borrow something, even if she were uncomfortable about being beholden to her new sister-in-law. Or even more beholden, she thought to herself with a grimace she tried to hide.

She must not have hidden it, or her husband was keeping an eagle's eye on her. He asked her if all was well.

"Perfectly fine, thank you. I'll just be happy to not be in constant motion." She managed to come up with her reply quickly.

"Was it perfectly dreadful? Ella didn't say too much about the train ride when she went west." Sybil's tone was solicitous.

"I wouldn't say dreadful," Jane began. "But the constant motion does get trying after a while. I would have to have a very pressing reason to be willing to get back on a train any time too soon. But I think it's much better than the oxen-drawn wagons that people used to have to take to get that far west. I do believe that's how Carter travelled west."

Sybil produced an exaggerated shudder, bringing a giggle from Jane. "I barely remember Carter," Sybil said. "But from what I recall, he was always up for a lark. He probably thought it was a grand adventure."

"I'm sure he did. He was a young man, on his own. It probably *was* a grand adventure. And it has certainly paid off for him. He and Ella are well settled and very happy."

"But I do wish they would visit sometime," Sybil complained.

"Perhaps they will. The train seems to be becoming more and more reliable. We didn't have any trouble at all. Perhaps it will even become faster, although I can barely imagine that."

"Oh, I do hope they will visit."

"Don't expect it to be too soon, though," Jane cautioned. "You do know Ella is expecting, don't you?"

Another funny expression crossed Sybil's face. "Yes, I received a letter about that recently. She does seem to be excited about it."

"Of course," Jane said. "But I don't expect they would want to travel with a baby, at least not right away."

Sybil pulled a face. "Perhaps I will just have to pluck up my courage and go see them, in that case."

"Ella would be thrilled to receive you," Jane answered promptly.

"Isn't it so funny that I've never met you, but you're friends with my best friend?" Sybil remarked as her eyes examined Jane's face. "I must say, though, now that the first excitement is past, you do look familiar. Have we met? Did we perhaps go to school together?

You are from Boston, aren't you? There's a good chance our paths have crossed at some point."

"Oh, no, I don't think so. Surely, we were from other sides of town from one another." Jane's heart sank at the thought of everything coming out when she had just arrived. She had just begun to feel comfortable with Alastair, and she desperately wanted him and his sister to grow fond of her. Surely, if they cared for her, they'd be willing to forgive her past mistakes.

Sybil was still gazing at her with a frown. "It'll probably come to me in the middle of the night one of these nights," she said. "Don't you just hate it when you can't think of what you're trying to remember?"

Jane knew her smile was thin, but she tried to make it genuine. She sincerely hoped her new sister would never remember Jane's real smile or why her face looked familiar. Jane reassured herself that her resemblance to Phoebe was minimal. Sybil never had to know.

Chapter Ten

Fred couldn't believe how smoothly his wife seemed to be adjusting to his life. She was a lovely girl. Woman, really. He didn't know how to refer to her even in his own head. But she was lovely. And he was relieved to see that she was taking Sybil in her stride. Fred hadn't expected his sister to be at the train station, although he probably should have. He had wired to tell her which train they were on, just so she wouldn't be worried about him. But he should have realized she would take that as an invitation to welcome them home.

They had always been close. He should be grateful she seemed so happy to meet his wife. She could have decided to be jealous. Even though she was married, she had maintained her close bond with her brother, and she could begrudge the obvious need he will have to divert his own attention toward his wife. But it didn't seem like that was happening. Not that he would expect his sister to be the jealous type, but he knew females could be contrary creatures at times. Even his new wife could take it into her head not to appreciate his sister's presence. But Jane didn't seem to mind, even if she appeared to be a little dazed by Sybil's energetic flitting about.

Once they had arrived at his house, Sybil had completely taken over. Perhaps Fred should have insisted that she not be there for his wife's first introduction to his house. He wanted her to feel at home there. Having Sybil show it to her might make it feel like it's another woman's home. Fred watched closely to monitor what his wife might be thinking.

Perhaps she was too tired. Jane seemed to be keeping a tight grip on her feelings. Fred couldn't really tell what was going through her mind. But Sybil had been right. He did want to go in to work. It was like an itch. But he also longed to spend more time with his wife. One would think he'd had enough of her after six days of constant togetherness. But it seemed like the more time he spent with her, the more time he wanted to spend with her. Perhaps he could interest Jane in his office, he thought before rejecting the idea, at least for the time being. He didn't want Sybil at his office. She was great, but her exuberance would only slow down productivity rather than help it. And it didn't seem as though they'd be able to rid themselves of Sybil any time soon. Fred felt guilty for the disloyal thought.

"Will you two be all right without me if I just run over to the office for an hour or two?"

Jane's smile looked a little strained to Fred's untrained eye, but she nodded along with Sybil. "We shall be fine, don't worry about us. Your sister seems excited to show me all the domestic sides of the house, which might be more interesting for me than for you."

"I do love this house. I wouldn't mind showing those things to you."

Jane tilted her head as though examining him. "Would you like us to wait for you then?"

Fred shook his head; he was being foolish. But a part of him worried that if he left his wife behind, that somehow the comfortable amicability he and Jane had established would somehow disappear.

"No, no, you are probably right to exclude me. If you're certain you won't feel abandoned if I leave for a bit, I'll try to return as quickly as possible."

Fred could have sworn Jane looked worried, but she merely shook her head and smiled at him. "Go ahead. I'll be here when you come back."

"Be sure that you are," he said with mock severity. Fred was suddenly struck with the thought that he didn't even know how to take leave of his wife. In that moment, he wished his sister to perdition. They didn't need a witness for their awkward leave taking. Ought he to kiss her? Hug her? Shake her hand?

He quickly kissed Jane's cheek and hurried from the room with his sister's giggles chasing him from the house.

~~~

"I think Fred mixed us up," Sybil said when she got her laughter under control.

Jane wasn't sure what her sister-in-law had found so funny. Her confusion must have been plain to see.

Sybil explained. "He usually kisses my cheek when taking his leave. I was expecting to witness an
~~~

embarrassing display of affection, but instead I didn't even get a farewell."

Jane had to laugh at Sybil's comical dismay, but she had been grateful that Alastair hadn't drawn out the awkward moment. She hurried to change the subject.

"Why do you continue to call him Fred?"

Sybil blinked at her. "Why wouldn't I? Have you taken to calling him Alastair?" She peeled off into giggles again. "Does he answer you when you do?"

Jane felt heat climbing her cheeks but refused to be cowed by the siblings' closeness. She kept her chin raised. "He does, as a matter of fact. I asked for his preference, and he said he would like me to call him Alastair. That is his name."

"Well, I suppose it is, but no one calls him that."

"I do." Jane kept her reply firm but decided to change the subject and keep the peace, as she saw it didn't please the other woman. Jane wasn't sure if she should think of her as her guest or her host. This lovely home was more familiar to the other woman, even though Jane was married to its owner. "Shall we have some tea?"

"Oh dear, I forgot to let your housekeeper know to return. Did you think to send her a telegram?"

Jane shrugged. "I didn't know we had a housekeeper."

Sybil laughed again. "Of course, you do. How else would you keep up with the house?"

Jane didn't know how to answer, hoping it was a rhetorical question. "Surely we can manage for ourselves today. Alastair will know what to do about staff."

Sybil's laughter cooled with Jane's use of Alastair's name, but she stood and led the way from the room. "I haven't made tea in ages, but I do know my way to the kitchen."

"I've gotten quite good at it, so you can be my guest. If you take it how Ella likes it, we'll do well."

"Were you making Ella's tea?"

"Very few women have household staff out West," was all Jane could think to say.

Thankfully, Sybil didn't seem to be one to stay miffed, and she quickly started prattling on about various social engagements while Jane made herself at home in the kitchen. It was beautiful in her opinion. Well-appointed and clean. She rather thought she would enjoy cooking in the room. But perhaps Alastair would think it beneath her to do something so domestic.

Jane stifled her sigh. He hadn't seemed the sort to be like that. He hadn't made a single disparaging comment about Ella's kitchen or their cooking while they were at the McLains', but things here in the city were sure to be different. Jane resolved to ask him as soon as he returned. While he hadn't seemed to want her to find work outside the home, perhaps he wouldn't object to her taking on domestic duties within their own house.

Jane tried not to sigh, as she didn't really want Sybil asking about it, but she couldn't help being a little saddened over her turn of circumstances. It was foolish, she knew, to be sad about being so elevated from where she had been. But she understood where she stood as an employee. For her, right now, her life seemed precarious. What was going to happen if her husband or her sister-in-law found out what she had done? And even if they didn't, what if their friends found out she had once been the help? Would Alastair be ostracized? Would all her lovely new circumstances disappear? Would he lose his house? His job? Would she have to return to scrubbing floors? Not that she would mind so very much, but she couldn't envision her husband falling in love with her after that.

Putting the disquieting thoughts aside, Jane tried to concentrate on what Sybil was chattering about. The other woman seemed sweet and kind, but she sure could talk a lot.

"So, will you join me?"

Jane blinked. She hadn't caught the beginning part where the pertinent details were contained. She smiled even if it was forced.

"I'll have to check with your brother, first, I'm afraid. Our lives together are still so new. I'm sure you understand."

A fretful expression crossed Sybil's face. "No, I don't really understand. Fred will allow you to do whatever you'd like. I'm sure of it."

Jane stared at her sister-in-law, unsure what to make of her bitter tone. "While you might be right, I still don't think I should make a commitment without discussing it with him, especially if it might involve any sort of expense."

Sybil continued to gaze at her with a degree of resentment, and Jane was filled with fear that the other woman had realized who she was. But then she seemed to deflate right before Jane's eyes.

"I'm sorry, Jane, you are probably in the right of it, and I'm being silly. While I have a certain relationship with Fred and it's strange to think of him as a husband, your relationship with him will be different from mine, and I will have to respect that. And if you want to be the sort of wife who asks her husband about every little thing, that's probably sweet, too. I don't have that sort of relationship with my husband, but we're slightly broken at the best of times, so I shouldn't compare."

Jane made a small sound of distress, and Sybil's face brightened. "Oh, don't feel too much sympathy for me. I was young and foolish and made a great mistake. But we're trying to make the most of it. Perhaps if I started sharing my thoughts and feelings with him more he'd appreciate that and it wouldn't be so dreadful."

"Do you think he'd be receptive to hearing your thoughts and feelings?" Jane wasn't quite sure what Sybil was trying to say, and she also didn't know if she should be prying into the matter. But she couldn't ignore what the other woman had said.

Sybil shrugged. "He hasn't been in the least concerned with my thoughts in the past, but he has been making an effort to be different lately. He is much more careful in what he says to me ever since Fred explained a few things to him."

"It was kind of your brother to get involved." Jane wasn't so sure if it was, but she didn't know what else to say. She wouldn't have felt like she could say anything to Phoebe's husband, but then he treated his wife way better than she even deserved. Perhaps if he hadn't, she would have felt obligated to say something. And then again, she wasn't a man. This thought struck her as comical, but she didn't want Sybil to think she was amused by her situation, so she quickly stifled her thoughts.

"It was kind of him, I suppose. I've been begging him to do something for years, but he has always refused to get involved until he—" With that, Sybil quickly stopped herself, going so far as to cover her mouth and look at Jane with wide eyes. "Never mind, don't tell him I said anything. I didn't say anything, so there's nothing to tell, is there?"

Jane watched in surprise as the other woman sipped back the rest of her tea and got to her feet, almost in one flowing move.

"So, discuss it with Fred and have a message sent to me if you do want to go shopping tomorrow. I'll be available most of the day, so whatever time is most convenient for you, just let me know."

That answered what Jane had missed in the conversation, but she was left standing, trailing behind her sister-in-law as she beat a hasty retreat from the house.

Blinking in the silence that was left in her wake, Jane stood in the foyer and looked around. She was alone in the house. It both thrilled and terrified her. She could explore on her own, which would be the best way to see it, without anyone judging her reactions or interrupting her interests in mysterious ways.

But where to start? She had already seen the kitchen, but even getting there and back was a bit of a blur, since she had been following in Sybil's wake. With a smile, Jane decided to start at the bottom and make her way to the top.

Poking her nose into every nook and cranny of the not overly large house, Jane was satisfied that she would be happy to make this home. Whether Alastair would insist upon hired help or not, Jane felt capable of caring for the house. Of course, with a maid or two, it would be easy, even if children joined the household. There was certainly room. The bottom, besides the kitchen, held sufficient storage space that wasn't yet crammed with too many things.

Jane wondered how long Alastair had been living in the house. It appeared to have been purchased rather than inherited. She doubted it was the house he had grown up in. There wouldn't be any available space in the storage rooms or cupboards if it hadn't been vacated at some time in the not too distant past. But she also didn't think it was brand new. It held that comfortable air of having been lived in. Jane quite liked it. It was grander than anything she had lived in since she was a small child, but not too grand that she wouldn't be able to feel at home.

The main floor, where guests would be entertained, held three large rooms. It would be perfect if they ever entertained, or when their family grew. One room, which was obviously the one preferred by Alastair, as it was the only one that appeared to be used at all, contained more books than Jane had ever seen all in one house. Two full walls were covered in books, and there was even a ladder so you could climb to the top of the shelves. There was a comfortable looking window seat that would be perfect for curling up and enjoying the contents of those shelves. She hoped Alastair would continue to tolerate her presence, as she had every intention and desire to read as many of those books as she could. Perhaps if she read enough books, she would stop lamenting her lack of education and no one would need ever know.

Shaking her head at her own ridiculous concerns, Jane continued her explorations. The next floor had four comfortably sized bedrooms and sufficient cupboards and storage that she felt reasonably confident that, even with children in the house, she would be able to keep it tidy and free of clutter. There was one more door that was a little difficult to open, but she managed it with a good tug. It opened onto a narrow staircase. Jane thought back to her first glimpses of the exterior of the house and suspected this led to the attic.

A shiver ran down her spine as she wondered what might be contained in the obviously seldom-used space. Creeping up the stairs, Jane was surprised when she got to the top that it was just another floor of the house. The slanted roof made it seem far less spacious than the other floors, but it would be usable space should they require it. Either if their family grew exceptionally, or if they needed to house any hired help.

From what she had seen thus far, it didn't appear as though anyone but Alastair lived in the house. And now she, too, she supposed, although she had yet to actually move in. She wondered where she ought to place the bags Alastair had left at the bottom of the stairs. She hurried down from the attic space, being careful to close the door tightly as she had found it. This did not feel like her home yet. She needed to leave everything precisely as she found it.

Just as she reached the bottom of the stairs, she heard the front door opening. Jane felt the flutter of a million butterflies as she was about to welcome her handsome husband home for the first time. Would he be glad to have her there or wish he were coming home to the quiet of his empty house?

Chapter Eleven

Fred's face broke into a grin when he saw Jane hovering at the base of the stairs.

"Well, hello. Were you waiting for me?"

"In a manner of speaking." Jane laughed as she made the uninformative comment. Fred merely raised his eyebrows, and she quickly explained, much to his delight. "Sybil had to rush away, so I've been exploring on my own. It felt deliciously mischievous to be snooping about by myself."

"Did Sybil not show you around? Oh, Jane, I'm so sorry. I should never have gone off to work on our first day here."

Fred's heart sank. He had failed his new wife less than a week into their acquaintance. He was stopped from berating himself overly, though, by her peel of laughter.

"I beg you, don't feel badly. It was actually perfect. I was able to poke and prod without feeling judgment from anyone. I think I would have felt awkward being shown around by your sister. And perhaps even if you had given me a tour. Now, I know where everything is, and we needn't worry about it."

"Well, I appreciate your sunny view of the matter, but why did Sybil leave you like that? She had seemed so anxious to spend the day with you. I had thought she would still be here when I arrived."

"Are you disappointed?"

Fred heard an odd note in his wife's voice but couldn't identify it.

"Not in the least, to be honest with you. Isn't it dreadful? I love my sister, of course, but in the week that I've known you, I've come to realize that your company is far more restful than hers. I thought it was all females. Now I realize my sister is flighty."

Jane giggled, bringing a smile to Fred's face.

"I don't know if I would call her flighty," Jane started in a measured tone. "But I, too, was surprised when she hurried off. It seemed to me as though she were about to divulge a secret and was so upset at her slip that she had to take herself to task."

Fred's heart sank anew. He should have known Sybil couldn't keep a secret.

"What kind of secret?"

"Well, I have no way of knowing, now do I? Besides, if she was that upset about it, I probably shouldn't have even told you that much. But I don't want to keep secrets from you, so I thought I ought to tell you, even though I actually don't know anything." Jane followed up her convoluted explanation with another giggle. "That made no sense whatsoever, did it? I must be more tired than I realized."

Fred continued to feel like a heel. He hadn't seen to his wife's needs.

"Have you eaten anything? Is it just you in the house? Have you met Mrs. Baker?"

He loved how Jane stared at him blinking while she pondered what he had said. She smiled gently as she tried to answer all his questions.

"I'm pretty sure I'm the only one here. I looked in every single room and didn't come across another being. Not even a cat, I was surprised to note. And, no, I haven't yet eaten. I wasn't sure when you would be coming back, so I didn't know if I should cook us something. And really, to be honest, I had just finished snooping when you arrived home. I was just about to contemplate where to put our baggage when you came through the door."

Fred glanced at the luggage she had indicated and then back at her face. Her usually highly expressive face was smoothed into an effort to not reveal her discomfort. He appreciated her attempt, he supposed, although he would prefer if she would confide in him. Smiling, he bent down and picked both pieces up.

"Did you decide which room you'd like to stay in for the time being?" He asked the question as he approached the stairs, but he was watching her closely from the corner of his eye and was relieved to see a smile stretch her face.

"I was torn between the front room with the lovely yellow paper and the room in the back with the cozy window seat. The yellow room seems like it would be so cheerful to wake up in, but the back room would be very comfortable to spend time in."

"Why not alternate? We aren't likely to have any overnight guests in the coming days, so you can sleep in every room in the house, if you have a mind for it."

"Oh, good heavens, no, that would make too much work with the bedding."

"Mrs. Baker won't mind."

Fred stifled his amusement as Jane's mouth opened and closed as she tried to formulate a response to his comment. Finally, she settled on asking a question.

"Who is Mrs. Baker?"

"She is our housekeeper. You will like her, I'm sure. She's a pleasant woman, a fair bit older than you, I'd say. Her children are grown, anyhow. She's been looking after me for the past year. Helped me move in here a few weeks ago."

"A few weeks? I thought it didn't seem as though it had been lived in long. There's nothing in storage," she explained at his obviously questioning look. "Where did you live before?"

She was trailing behind him up the stairs as they talked. Fred was glad she couldn't see his face. They were getting too close to the things he didn't want to tell her about.

"I was renting rooms before. Mrs. Baker would come in and cook and clean for me two days a week, but she said she would be more than happy to work more days for me once I bought the house. I actually brought her to see it before I made my final decision. She said the kitchen was a dream."

Jane laughed. "I thought the exact same thing when I saw it. But she hasn't stocked it much. I didn't have any trouble finding things for tea, but there wasn't much else."

"I sent her to visit her daughter while I went out West to collect you," Fred explained. "There was no sense her rattling around in the empty house when she could be enjoying herself instead."

"That was kind of you."

Fred laughed. "It also saved me from having to pay her."

"Oh, that sounds sneaky."

Fred was surprised how much her remark hurt. He had come to enjoy her good opinion. "I did buy her ticket to New York."

"Well, I suppose that's good then."

"I should have thought to tell her to meet us here. I thought Sybil would have done it, since she was watching the train schedule so closely."

"We can manage just fine without her. I'd be happy to keep house for you."

"I don't want you working yourself into exhaustion." Fred felt beholden to his wife and didn't want her tiring herself out on his behalf.

Jane shrugged. "It doesn't seem to me that you'll be too much trouble. If you couldn't stay away from your office on your first day home, I have a feeling you aren't likely to be home much. And cooking for two isn't much work at all."

"Very well, then you can start in the morning. For now, let's go get ourselves fed at the alehouse, and then we can stop and pick up whatever you think we might need. I'm fairly certain Mrs. Baker has things delivered, but she probably had that cancelled while we were going to be away for an uncertain length of time."

"Did you think it was going to take you a long time to collect me?" Jane's question was accompanied by laughter, so Fred didn't think she was upset about it.

He shrugged. "I really didn't know what I would encounter out West, to be honest. Perhaps you would have been reluctant to leave. Perhaps the travel would have been more complicated than expected. Perhaps I would have loved it out there and wouldn't have wanted to return. There was really no way to know how long I'd be."

Jane nodded as though she understood. But then Fred added one more perhaps. "It was even possible I wouldn't make it back alive. Accidents happen so very easily while travelling."

Her loud gasp was satisfying until her eyes filled with tears. Fred shook his head at his own foolishness. "I'm so sorry, Jane, I shouldn't have said that." But he was too late. He had thought his wife was firm and steady, but here she was, dissolved into a fit of sobbing.

Standing there feeling helpless, Fred wasn't certain what he should do. They were standing in the open space between the four bedrooms. He dropped the baggage he was still holding and pulled his wife's trembling form into his arms. She made a sound of protest but didn't pull away. Fred rather suspected she were protesting her own breakdown and his witness of it rather than his offer of comfort.

Of course, he felt dreadful for making her cry, but holding her in his arms was the most comfortable sensation he had felt in ages, perhaps ever. His heart thudded as he thought about the fact that this lovely young woman was his wife. She would remain by his side, and they would build a life together.

He pulled his thoughts back to the matter at hand. He wasn't quite sure why his wife was so beside herself. He hadn't actually been serious about harm coming to him or to them or whatever she seemed to be so concerned about. And clearly, it hadn't happened anyway, even if he had thought it might. They were both hale and hearty and perfectly fine. He might even consider train travel again in the future.

She was trying to speak in between her sobs, but Fred was having difficulty making out what exactly she was saying. From the sounds of it, her upset might have more to do with Sybil than with his silly remark about dying. Fred had thought Jane had said her visit with his sister had gone well but obviously, it hadn't if she was this upset. Finally, after another moment, she managed to get herself back under control. He produced a handkerchief from one of his pockets, which elicited a watery chuckle from the lovely package in his arms.

"That was unexpected," Fred said.

She answered with another chuckle. This one seemed a little more real.

"I think perhaps you are just beside yourself with hunger and exhaustion. Might that be the case?" He couldn't see her face, but he felt her nod as her hair brushed his chin. His heart lurched again as he felt how perfectly she fit with him.

"Come along then. Let's get ourselves fed, and everything will seem much more right with the world."

"Thank you, Alastair. I'm sorry for turning into a watering pot on you. I'll just run and wash my face, and then I'll be ready to go."

"Take all the time you need."

~ ~ ~

Jane ran down to the kitchen where she knew for sure there was a source of water. She felt like a ninny. How foolish to manage to hold herself together for days on end only to fall apart at one misspoken word. If she didn't watch out, she would be divulging every last secret she possessed, and then she would find herself out on the streets for her trouble.

Making quick work of cleaning up, Jane hurried back up the stairs to find her husband waiting for her by the front door.

"All better now?"

Jane almost snorted over his question but managed to keep that contained, offering him a smile in the hopes that he would take that for a yes. Because it was certainly not all better. It was much, much worse. She was in love with her husband. And she was keeping secrets from him. Big ones. Ones that could end their relationship before it had even really begun. And that was just the most foolish mistake she had yet made in her mistake-riddled life. A sigh was struggling to come up from the depths of her soul, but she managed to swallow it down.

She would do her very best not to allow her husband to read her thoughts, and she prayed she would have herself well under control by the morning. Maybe Alastair was right and it was just hunger and a lack of sleep making her so very melancholy. But she feared it was more than that. Her secrets were pushing at her conscience. She wasn't sure she would be able to contain them much longer.

It was a short walk around the corner to the eating house. Jane had never been to one before and was thrilled at the thought of eating something prepared by strangers.

It would seem Alastair found her fascination amusing. "Have you truly never been to an eating house or a restaurant?"

Jane knew her face was flushing but what could she say? "No, never. The closest I've come was the food on the train."

"Well, I guess that is very similar, isn't it?"

"Yes, but it is necessary on the train. Here it seems all the more luxurious because you aren't obliged to come. Do you know what I mean? We have a kitchen, and I'm perfectly fit. We weren't obliged to come to the eating house. It is a luxury. And I intend to enjoy every last drop of it."

Alastair laughed again. "Well, I hope it actually suits your tastes. I eat here regularly, and it's just simple food."

Jane laughed, too. "I always enjoy any meal I haven't had to prepare myself."

"You're still so young to have been responsible for so long." Alastair's observation made Jane squirm in her seat and quickly change the subject.

"Might I ask why you come here regularly? I thought you said Mrs. Baker cooks for you."

"Oh, she does, but like I said, I've only been having her a few days each week. She will start working for us every day, now that you're here."

Jane's flush deepened. "That isn't necessary, Alastair. Surely, I can manage a few chores and meals."

She couldn't interpret the expression that flitted across his face as he assured her, "I owe it to you, my dear. And as you said, we might have a family for you to look after before too very long. I would rather you enjoy yourself in the meantime."

Jane still wasn't convinced she would know what to do with herself without a job to go to or friends to spend time with, but she wasn't about to argue the topic. Thankfully, at that moment their food was delivered and they were too busy partaking to continue the conversation.

"You were definitely correct, Alastair. I was famished and didn't even realize."

"Was the food all right?" He sounded anxious, which Jane found endearing.

"It was perfect, thank you. I fear you are being far too kind to me."

Alastair laughed. "That's hardly possible."

Jane climbed the stairs ahead of her husband, intent upon her own thoughts and feelings. She felt a desperate need to bare her secrets to Alastair.

Fred was just about to follow his wife up the few stairs to his front door when he heard himself being hailed from a distance.

"Fred, wait, don't go in there."

Turning, he was surprised to see Sybil dashing toward him, her hair and coat flowing behind her.

"What happened to you? What are you doing out so late?"

"I couldn't allow you to spend even one more night with that viper you have brought back into our lives."

Fred felt his face falling in shock and dismay over his sister's words.

"I beg your pardon? What has gotten into you? Are you unwell? You aren't speaking about my wife in this manner, are you?"

"I most certainly am, and you're going to agree with me when I tell you what I know."

Fred stared at Sybil before glancing up at his door. What should he do? He couldn't stand on the street debating the merits of his marital choice. "Come inside and explain yourself, Sybil. We can't stay here making a scene."

Indecision pressed upon Sybil's features before they hardened into determination. "Very well, Fred, I'd like to tell that woman exactly what I think of her."

"Now Sybil, do try to be reasonable for a moment. Don't forget how very much we owe her."

Sybil sniffed. "If not for her, I wouldn't have needed any assistance."

Fred opened his mouth to answer but shut it with a snap. He didn't know what she was talking about, but he didn't want to air any grievances on the street for any nosy neighbors to consider. His sister was excitable at the best of times, but now she seemed truly beside herself. He didn't bother making any further comment, merely ushered her up the stairs and into the house.

Jane obviously hadn't heard the exchange, as she was standing at the base of the stairs with an expectant air of inquiry. Fred couldn't prevent the increase of his heart rate and the warmth that flooded him at seeing her warm smile despite his sister's strange behavior.

"Welcome home," she greeted in a somewhat shy tone before looking past him with a slightly puzzled expression. "Welcome back, Sybil, I didn't think to see you again this evening."

"You probably hoped to never see me again, didn't you? Did you think we wouldn't find out about your perfidy?"

Fred was shocked to see all color drain from his wife's face, and the guilt that was written on her features surprised him even further. It would seem Jane had some idea of what his sister was raving about.

"Shall we adjourn to the sitting room and discuss this like civilized people?" Fred suggested with a calm he didn't quite feel.

"I do not wish to speak with her," Sybil fairly spat the words. "And she isn't civilized."

"Sybil," Fred began with a warning tone. "Jane is my wife, and this is her home. I would ask that you speak in a respectful manner."

"That woman doesn't deserve my respect, Fred. And you will agree with me when I tell you what I know."

Jane said nothing, merely sinking down to sit upon the stair she had been standing on. Fred transferred his worried gaze between her and his sister, torn between wondering who he ought to turn to first. Since Sybil was the one making noise, she drew his attention.

"I finally remembered why her face looked so familiar, Fred. She used to work for Horace's mother."

Fred blinked, glancing at Jane in surprise. "You worked for Mrs. Trenton?"

She nodded slightly.

"It was she who started the rumors about me that led to my marriage with Horace."

"I'm afraid I still don't understand."

"If not for her, my marriage with Horace most likely would never have happened." Sybil's voice was high and shrill, making Fred worry for her, but he turned to Jane for some sort of explanation or denial. His wife merely gazed back at him with bleak eyes.

"That is enough, Sybil. I would ask that you await me in the vestibule. You ought to return home. I will escort you, but I need to speak with Jane a moment."

"Don't let her turn your head, Fred. She's a viper, I'm telling you."

"That's enough, I said. Await me in the vestibule."

Fred didn't wait for further argument from her. He was gentle as he grasped Jane's arm, but he felt her flinch anyway. Turmoil nearly engulfed him as he towed his wife into the sitting room to afford them a degree of privacy. He would have to see to his sister, but he owed his wife the courtesy of hearing her out first.

"She's not lying to you. Your sister's dreadful marriage *is* my fault. I did used to work for Mrs. Trenton."

"How did you come to be in service for the Trentons?" Fred's disbelief was palpable.

"A couple months after my mother died, my father told me I needed to help the family. He had found me a position with a household as a kitchen helper."

"But weren't you a small child when your mother died?" It was as though Alastair couldn't keep up with her story.

"Yes, but that didn't preclude me finding a position."

"No, of course not, but why did everyone suddenly have to work?"

"It wasn't everyone. My brothers and sister stayed in school. I'm fairly certain my father continued to work, at least for a time, but he took to drinking too much after Mother died, and her family cast us off."

"Why would your mother's family cast you off?"

"Remember, I was a child, so I didn't understand any of it at the time. But from what I understand now, they never approved of my mother's choice in marrying my father. For some reason, they blamed him for her death. She died in childbirth along with the little boy she was birthing. So I suppose in a roundabout way you could say it was my father's fault, but that wasn't really fair to any of us. Not that we were their responsibility, of course, but I think they must have paid some of the household expenses while Mother was alive, and they stopped doing so afterward. Or perhaps they owned the house we lived in. I never did find out the truth about that, but suddenly we were in very poor surroundings."

She paused, taking a shaky breath before continuing.

"As an adult, I can see that continuing in school must have been a challenge for my brothers and sister with such a drastic change in their circumstances, but I was heartbroken to not be able to continue my schooling."

"I still don't understand why you, as the youngest child, were the one expected to help support the family. And what does all of this have to do with Sybil and Horace?"

Jane's face flamed with embarrassment. Alastair's tone was kind, as though he were trying to understand, but she knew he would be angry once she managed to get to the point.

"Phoebe always wanted to fit in with her friends. This got worse for her after our circumstances changed so much. She loved to gossip. She would tell tales about anyone and everyone."

As Jane was talking, she didn't want to look at Alastair, but she couldn't prevent herself from watching for his reaction. His understanding was slowly dawning.

"It was Phoebe who spread the tales about Sybil that made her marry Horace?"

Jane nodded. "I only found out about it afterward. I didn't really know Horace, and I had never met Sybil, but I had one day each week to visit my family, and I must have said something about them that Phoebe misconstrued and spread around."

"Forcing my sister into her disastrous marriage," Alastair concluded for her, his tone cooling as he watched her.

Jane had cried so hard before they went out to eat, she didn't have any tears left. She was filled with despair as she watched the happy life she had almost grasped slipping away. Alastair got to his feet and paced away from her.

"Of all the women in all the world, how could I end up married to the only one responsible for setting my sister into such an unhappy life? I've always thought it was my fault. But all along it was yours. I know it is really Phoebe's fault, but if not for you, she wouldn't have had the ammunition to use against Sybil."

As he talked he seemed to get more and more angry. Jane cringed as he approached her.

"I can barely look at you right now." His voice was so cold. "And I'm sure to say more than I ought to. I need to see my sister home. I will stay with her tonight. We'll figure out what to do with ourselves tomorrow."

Jane couldn't even speak. She didn't blame him. She could barely stand herself, so she couldn't expect him to understand how desperately she wanted her family's approval. It hadn't only been Phoebe who would do anything to fit in. Jane had worked her fingers to the bone to provide for her family, but it had never seemed to be enough. She had never meant any harm to anyone, but the only time Phoebe seemed to enjoy her company was when Jane was telling her about the people she worked for. Jane was horrified when she had eventually realized how Phoebe had used the information.

If Jane had ever considered that Ella would marry her off to the one man in all the world she didn't want to marry, she never would have signed the proxy papers. But Ella hadn't even mentioned Alastair's name. And Jane hadn't suspected Alastair Fredericksburg could ever possibly be in the business of matchmaking.

When she heard the front door slam, Jane stared toward it for a long moment. This was not at all how she had expected the first night in her new home to turn out. As it happened, it was also probably going to be the last night.

She had been longing for a solid bed that had no movement, but she hadn't expected to be trying to sleep as the only person in a big, empty house. Jane had thought she had no tears left to shed, but she was proven wrong as she cried herself to sleep.

Chapter Twelve

After a fitful night, Fred stared down at the street from his sister's sitting room.

"What are you going to do, Fred?" He was glad to hear that his sister sounded far less hysterical than she had the night before.

"I need to go home, Sybil. I shouldn't have left her behind like that. I'm dreadfully sorry for everything that has happened over the past five years, but I have a responsibility toward her now. You aren't my only concern anymore."

"Are you abandoning me?" Fred was grateful to hear there was actually a touch of humor in her tone as she asked.

"Don't ask such a daft question, Sybil. I've only abandoned you once, and you know I've vowed never to repeat that mistake."

Fred was surprised to see his sister's face crease into a wide grin. "I know, Fred, and in fact, you've never abandoned me."

"Sure I did, Sybil. If I had been here, instead of at school, I never would have let you be so affected by a few whispers."

Sybil shrugged. "You might not have been able to stop me, Fred. I was rather infatuated with Horace, you know that. It was the gossip that forced his hand. But at the time, I was glad of it." She paused for a moment in reflection. "I don't envy you being attached, even if just through marriage, to that Phoebe women, but I can see now that it really wasn't Jane's fault. As you said, she was a child, forced into service, trying to gain the affection of her big sister. I can relate to trying to impress a sibling."

Fred shared an affectionate glance with his sister before he returned his attention to the street outside. "Are you going to be able to accept her?" He paused to allow her to answer, but he continued when she remained silent. Not wanting to pressure Sybil, Fred didn't even look at her when he asked, "I do not think, as a man of honor, that I could abandon her, even though she kept this from me. I feel wretched as it is that I left her as I did. She must be beside herself by now."

"I doubt Jane is in hysterics, Fred. She struck me as a remarkably steady young woman."

This brought Fred's gaze back to his sister. "Seems to me, you can't be holding much of a grudge against her if you're able to defend her in this way."

Sybil shrugged. "I had a chance to sleep on it. As you said, she was a child prattling to her older sister. She wasn't trying to hurt me. And can you really blame her for keeping it to herself? If she even knew what her sister had done or what it had resulted in, what good is it to bring it all up now? Besides all that, you're keeping a rather big secret from her as well."

A wave of guilt swamped Fred suddenly.

"I'm going home."

Sybil trailed after him toward the door. "If she doesn't want to see you after you left her like that, you're always welcome here."

Fred couldn't get away fast enough. What if Sybil's words were true? What if Jane couldn't forgive him for acting the cad? He wanted to run home but managed to keep himself to a reasonable walk. Still, he was out of breath by the time he finally reached his house. But then he hesitated as his fears crawled under his skin. The thought of Jane not forgiving him made his heart stutter in his chest. The feelings he already had for his wife far outmatched anything he had ever felt before, even the love he had for his sister paled in comparison. Did that mean he loved Jane? But what kind of love was it if he could abandon her at the first sign of trouble? He was a fool.

Shocked to see his hand trembling as it reached toward the door handle, Fred took himself to task. He needed to be strong, own up to his mistakes, come clean with his own secrets, and make her forgive him. How he was going to do that remained a mystery, but he would do the best he could. Resolved, he turned the knob and entered the house.

~ ~ ~

Jane wandered around the empty house until she found herself in the library. It was obviously the only room besides his bedchamber that Alastair used. It was also the only room that appeared to be fully furnished. A bubble of mirth rose in Jane at the thought. She, too, would want the library finished before any other room. But she shook her head. Truly, she had little in common with her husband. She shouldn't allow something so random as a mutual love of reading to fill her with ideas for a comfortable future.

Trailing her finger along a row of books, Jane was reading the titles when she heard the sounds of Alastair returning home. She froze for a moment, wondering if she ought to hide or confront him. Stiffening her spine, Jane decided she wasn't going to cower in fear. She wanted to find happiness in this marriage. She was a fellow human; she deserved to be treated with a modicum of respect, Jane reminded herself as she tried to steel her backbone for what was sure to be an ordeal. She had married him in good faith and hoped they could resolve their issues.

"Hello," she called from the top of the staircase.

"Good day, Jane. You look—" He paused, and she couldn't help a gasp of laughter.

"Don't bother finishing the sentence, Alastair. I'm afraid I haven't the stomach for lies, and I know you won't want to insult me."

His grin was wry. "I should have thought before beginning the sentence. I was instinctively glad to see you. But to be honest, you don't look like you slept well."

Jane shrugged and nodded. "I didn't. I had been looking forward to sleeping in a bed that was firmly planted on a floor that doesn't move. But the events of the day wouldn't stop circling my mind."

"I know. I didn't fare any better."

A part of Jane wanted to lower her lashes and hide her shame. She had been meaning to make her confession, but had been interrupted by Sybil. She doubted Alastair would believe that at this point though. She felt badly about her part in the fiasco, but after a night of reflection, she didn't think she could be held accountable for another couple's marriage simply due to words she had uttered as a youngster. Jane gazed at her husband, waiting to see what he would say. Would he try to reconcile or would he tell her to go?

"I shouldn't have left you here by yourself last night. You were probably nervous."

Jane nodded. "It is surprisingly creaky in the middle of the night for such a lovely, new house."

Alastair smiled. "You do get used to it."

Jane wasn't sure if she would be there to find out. She decided in that moment not to wait for him to decide her fate. Grasping her courage in both hands and keeping her chin up, Jane asked the question that was most burning on her mind.

"Are you going to cast me off?"

"No, Jane, and I'm wretchedly sorry for even allowing you to think that was a possibility. I should never have left you here on your own yesterday, neither earlier in the day, and especially not last night. I'm ashamed of myself for doing so, and I hope you'll eventually be able to find it in yourself to forgive me."

Jane's heart soared at his words. Since she knew she loved her husband, she was fairly certain she would forgive him. Clearly, he seemed willing to forgive her.

Jane tried to keep her hopes under control. After the words that were spoken yesterday, she shouldn't be too certain of the man. She didn't know what to say in reply to his statement, so she merely offered him a smile. Jane feared it was a weak one, but it was the best she could muster.

"Could we go have a seat in the sitting room and talk?"

Jane wrinkled her nose. "I feel an aversion to that room, at the moment. Could we perhaps go to the library or even the kitchen? Would you like a cup of tea?"

Alastair chuckled, although it didn't have a great deal of mirth behind it. "Are you one of those people who thinks tea can solve everything?"

Jane laughed a little bit, too. "It's not necessarily the solution to every problem, but it doesn't hurt either."

"Very well, let us adjourn to the kitchen for some tea."

As Jane bustled around, stirring the fire and producing the kettle and tea bags, she watched from the corner of her eye as Alastair fidgeted, clearly still not comfortable with her. She sighed as she finally turned back toward him.

"You haven't said how Sybil is faring this morning."

"It's generous of you to ask after her."

Jane shrugged. "Not really. I feel badly about the situation and feel dreadful that she was so upset yesterday. It doesn't bode well for the future."

"She's remarkably recovered today and feels you ought to be reassured that she accepts that it really isn't your fault."

Jane blinked, surprised at the about face of the other woman.

Alastair grinned. "My sister is a little flighty, but you'll get used to her. And she can be delightful when she puts her mind to it."

Jane returned his smile as she poured the tea into their cups. The swirling steam curling into the air was a comfortingly familiar scent. Maybe everything *could* be solved with a cup of tea. She was startled by Alastair loudly clearing his throat. He sounded nervous. Jane brought her puzzled gaze to his face.

"I need to tell you about something. You aren't the only one that was keeping a secret. I haven't told you all the details surrounding our marriage."

Jane's stomach cramped. "What kind of details?"

Alastair reached out and clasped her hand. "Good ones, I promise, don't look so worried."

Trying not to think the worst, Jane nodded. "Very well, then, please tell me quickly so I can stop worrying."

Alastair fidgeted with his tea cup but kept hold of her hand, which Jane found comforting despite her fear.

"The thing is, I benefited greatly from our marriage."

Jane wrinkled her nose. "Do you mean because I'm such a catch?"

"Don't be sarcastic, Jane, you *are* a catch."

She didn't really believe him, but she appreciated his saying so. "I benefited from our marriage because it protected me from my sister's schemes. The husband she had picked out for me was a conniving fraudster, and I feared he wouldn't treat me well."

When Alastair winced, Jane hurried to add, "Perhaps you should just explain."

His laughter sounded nervous, but he complied. "In order to receive a rather large inheritance, I needed to be married. And I need to stay married for at least a year to receive the full amount."

Jane felt her jaw fall open in shock and tried to close it firmly. "You married me for money?" she asked as wild laughter pressed against her throat. "I've been feeling so horribly about this entire thing, and I even ran away because of my sister's schemes, and it has all been for money."

"Well, it isn't all about the money, Jane. I find I'm coming to care about you. I think we could have a good life together."

"How? I rather think that these things will always hang over us."

"Not if we don't let them, Jane. Please, try to understand."

Jane felt as though her heart were breaking once more. Once again, someone wanted her for what they could get from her. It was just like her father and her sister, and even the man Phoebe wanted her to marry. She felt the press of tears at the back of her lids and valiantly fought to keep them in check. Pulling her hand from Alastair's warm grasp, Jane rose to her feet.

"I'm going to have to think about this for a bit."

"We ought to talk about it, Jane, don't shut me out."

"You shut me out last night, Alastair. I'm just trying to catch up. I just need some time to adjust my thinking. I was hoping for a home."

Alastair wrinkled his forehead, not understanding her words. "We have a perfectly good house here. Do you want me to sell it and buy another one? Is it not big enough or to your taste?"

"This house is perfectly fine. But I don't want just a house. And certainly not one I'm required to live in so that my husband can secure his inheritance. I want a home filled with joy and laughter, not a house of sadness and obligation."

Alastair nodded. "I'll give you some time to think, then."

His face didn't reveal much of his thoughts, but Jane almost suspected that she had hurt his feelings. She scoffed at the thought and watched as he turned away from her and headed toward the stairs up to the bedrooms. She figured he was going to repack his bag. He would probably be going to his sister's again. It was for the best if it were him that went. Tears were pressing at the back of her eyelids. She hoped she could keep them contained until Alastair had left.

Chapter Thirteen

Fred was gathering a few items to put in his luggage, but his heart was sinking and his stomach felt like lead. This had been a disaster from the beginning. He should never have used the proxy Carter had sent him for himself. He should have found someone here in the city that he could trust and explain everything from the outset. And even if he had married Jane, he should have been honest with her from the start.

But the fact was, he didn't want to leave his wife. He quite liked her and rather thought he might love her. Fred could see a future with her, here in this house, with children running around and music and laughter filling all the empty spaces.

He threw his bag across the room and ran back down to the kitchen. Jane was still standing where he had left her, as though she had frozen to the spot by his thoughtless words and actions.

Fred strode toward her and grasped her shoulders.

"I don't want to leave this house. And I don't want you to leave it either."

Her confused expression brought a much-needed smile to his lips.

"All right, I don't mean not ever, but I want us to stay here together, Jane. I should never have kept things from you. We both knew this marriage was a convenience for each of us. You were open about why you needed it, but I allowed you to think I married you as a favor to Carter, and that was weak of me. I apologize."

Her wide, steady, wet gaze made his stomach flutter. He already had his hands on her, but he wanted to pull her to his chest and hold her there. He didn't do so, though, as he was afraid it would terrify her. He waited to see what she would say.

"Then, why didn't you?"

"Why didn't I what? Tell you the full story?"

"Yes, exactly. As you said, I clearly benefited from our marriage. Why didn't you tell me how much you benefited? Why did you want me to feel beholden to you?"

Fred's heart sank, and he felt the press of tears behind his own eyes. "I swear, I didn't want you to feel beholden to me. It's just that I didn't actually need the inheritance. I was doing very well for myself with my business. I didn't need the money. The inheritance has made it possible for me to gain control over Horace. My mother's sister was a sweet old lady, but she had strong notions. She was determined that I ought to be married. She always hated Horace, so she left all her money to me, rather than to Sybil. But she stipulated that I needed to be married and stay married to gain full access to the funds. I don't actually need any more money, although it is nice to be even more comfortable. But while I was well off before, I didn't have scads of extra that would allow me to manipulate Horace. Now, by offering him money with certain conditions, it has created a situation wherein he is treating Sybil much better."

He could tell Jane was listening attentively, but she still hadn't relaxed. She did seem convinced by his explanation. He continued. "It is a significant amount of money. And I've found people, women in particular, have treated me differently because of the money I already had. I preferred you to come to know me for me, not because of my bank account."

Her wide gaze finally filled with tears, and they started to slide down her cheeks. Fred couldn't take it anymore; he pulled her firmly in to his chest. Perhaps he was squeezing her too hard, but she didn't protest. And he had no intention of ever letting her go.

~ ~ ~

The thud of his heartbeat was sweet comfort as his strong arms held her tightly against his warm chest. Jane could stand there all day. All week, even. Frankly, she would like to never step away from her husband's warm embrace. She hadn't felt this cared for since she lost her mother. She realized she had given her heart into her husband's keeping somewhere between Indiana and Ohio. And just maybe he would be willing to hand his over into her care. The thought made her heart beat faster, and she snuggled closer into his chest.

His chuckle rumbled up into her ear.

"You're acting like a kitten searching for warmth."

Jane joined him in laughter. It was a good release for the pent-up feelings threatening to overwhelm her.

"The fact that you haven't pulled away or slapped my face gives me reason to hope you might give me a chance to make it up to you." Alastair's hopeful expression made the butterflies pick up their fluttering in between her stomach and her heart.

Grinning and nodding, Jane stepped back slightly to better see his face. Her heart soared when, instead of dropping his arms away from her, he went back to holding her shoulders.

"I guess we still have a lot to learn about each other. Perhaps we could just say that there hasn't been time to divulge everything and simply forgive the things that we might not have loved hearing about and move on." She said the words softly and held her breath to await his response.

Jane could feel his searching gaze scouring her face to ascertain her sincerity.

"Do you think you really can forgive this breach?"

She shrugged slightly. "Since you have no intention of abandoning me nor allowing me to abandon you, has there really been a breach? I'm sure there are many things I've yet to learn about you. But please, tell me this, are there any more large secrets looming?"

He shook his head.

"Are you completely certain? No children lurking in a basement I didn't yet come across? No former fiancés who shall be planning my demise?"

"No, I swear it, I haven't anything large or nasty in my past. And I shall make every effort to be an open book for you to peruse at your leisure."

"Did you know that reading is my greatest pleasure?"

"I had an inkling, my dear."

"I look forward to the reading of this particular book."

With a soft smile, Alastair's head started to descend toward hers. Jane tilted her face up to meet his. He was just a whisper away when he told her fervently, "I love you to the depths of my heart, Mrs. Jane Fredericksburg. If you'll allow me, I'd consider it an honor to court you."

Jane grinned. "Do you always do things backwards?"

"Not always," he replied before erasing her grin by placing his lips gently on hers.

Jane sighed into the kiss, releasing her grip on sanity. She had finally found home.

The End

If you enjoyed *A Wife for Alastair*, you'll also like the next book in this series:

A Wife for Hamilton

Marry in haste, repent at leisure...

Buy it through wendymayandrews.com

About the Author

I've been writing pretty much since I learned to read when I was five years old. Of course, those early efforts were basically only something a mother could love ☺ I put writing aside after I left school and stuck with reading. I am an avid reader. I love words. I will read anything, even the cereal box, signs, posters, etc. But my true love is novels.

Almost ten years ago my husband dared me to write a book instead of always reading them. I didn't think I'd be able to do it, but to my surprise I love writing. Those early efforts eventually became my first published book – Tempting the Earl (published by Avalon Books in 2010). There were some ups and downs in my publishing efforts. My first publisher was sold and I became an "orphan" author, back to the drawing board of trying to find a publishing house. It has been a thrilling adventure as I learned to navigate the world of publishing.

I believe firmly that everyone deserves a happily ever after. I want my readers to be able to escape from the everyday for a little while and feel upbeat and refreshed when they get to the end of my books.

When not reading or writing, I can be found traipsing around my neighborhood admiring the dogs and greenery or travelling the world with my favorite companion.

Stay in touch:

Website / Sign up for my newsletter

Facebook

Instagram

Twitter